On the Right Track

The Sullivans of Montana, Book 3

CHERYL BARTON

Dedication

To my number one cousin, Andrea Denise Gentry. May you continue to rest sweetly in heaven. Not many days go by that I don't think of you and the fun we would be having these days traveling and building wealth like we talked about. Thank you for the many late-night conversations in my little apartment on Radecke Avenue. You were my inspiration. You were my first sister! Those were the days! I miss you and love you, Cuz!

Prologue

The winning circle. Being lifted onto the shoulders of his pit crew and the exhilaration of being on top of his game once again had Dayton cheering along with everyone else in the stands and on the ground. He relished knowing that this was why he made the decision at the age of eighteen to become a professional racecar driver.

When loud calls of his last name, Sullivan, from over two hundred thousand attendees at the race filled the air, Dayton raised his fist in the air, looked to the sky and celebrated his family. He smiled, though they weren't in the stands, but were back home on the Sullivan Ranch in Bozeman, Montana, cheering, watching and celebrating his win. There was no doubt, his mother had been praying the whole race for his continued safety.

Being a racecar driver wasn't the safest profession he could have chosen, but everything about speed has been a part of him since he was a young boy riding dirt bikes and ATVs across the massive property that was the Sullivan Ranch.

Encouraging his team to put him down, Dayton had one focus and that was to find Kima and make sure they connect, even if it was only with their eyes.

As many around him continued to pat him on the back, he looked to where Kima usually sat, in the owner's box, since she and her father, Oscar, owned *TOBIT Motorsports*, the team he raced for. The happy smile left his face. Kima wasn't there. He'd seen her earlier when he first got into car in his signature blue, green and white fire-retardant suit and certified helmet. There was no way she could miss him since his attire was a sure way of picking him out of a crowd.

His suit, like everyone else's, served to identify him outside of his car, which had the same matching colors and signage of sponsors all over it. The suit also served to protect him in case of a car fire. He'd been on the other end of that a time or two, but not today. Today, he came through the race unscathed.

Removing his fire-retardant shoes and gloves, he heard a scream and looked toward the sound which pierced the sky, even over the continued hoop and hollering of the crowd. Then he saw her and something wasn't right. Kima was in his view, but what he saw disturbed him. She was being dragged across the concrete path that led to the parking lot. He saw a white van pull up and out jumped her father, Oscar, one of his slimy partners, Andrew Gaynor and Andrew's nerdy son, Nelson. Dayton tried to run to her at full speed but his feet wouldn't move. People were still milling about around him. He tried to push through them as he screamed out her name, but no one would move. Did no one else see and hear the terror in her voice?

Dayton looked down and his feet appeared to be set in cement. When did that happen? Could no one see that either? The scene terrified him. He couldn't breathe. His body began sinking as Kima's yells diminished in sound. He could no longer see or hear her as the van sped off. Still, he fought to get to her. He had to rescue Kima. She was the woman he loved and no one was going to take her away from him. His baby! What would happen to his child that Kima was carrying? He had to get to them – he had to fight his way through to her.

Fighting with all of his might, Dayton realized the harder he fought, the faster he began sinking into the cement which, as he looked down, the consistency changed instantly into quicksand. Why wasn't anyone helping him? Why were people still cheering as his woman was being kidnapped and he was sinking, dying right before their eyes. He continued to yell for Kima even as the filthy, gritty sand reached his shoulders. He grasped for anything in his reach. Finding a thick leg covered in black trousers, Dayton tried to hold on and pull himself up. When he looked up to beg the person to help him, he saw a groveling, sinister grin on Oscar's face. It was his leg that Dayton found himself grasping onto for dear life. The last thing he saw was the man lifting his other foot, placing it on the top of Dayton's head. With no one helping him, all the way into the cement Dayton went. Even his screams went unanswered as cheers continued to ring out for his win. He wasn't winning now.

"Day? Day? Wake up, baby! Day!"

Dayton sat straight up and scattered out of the bed, running his hands all over his body as if he were trying to swat at bugs that may have been crawling over his body. He couldn't control his breathing and then he knew; he had been dreaming. He wasn't drowning in cement that felt like quicksand. He didn't witness Kima being kidnapped and taken from him. The woman he would give his life for was with him. She still carried their child within her body.

Now aware of his surroundings, Dayton quickly got back into bed and pulled Kima so tight, he was afraid he was harming her. He peppered her face and neck with kisses and words of love. For him, this was a lot; showing this kind of affection for a woman, for any woman was new for him. The feeling of loss and dread over losing her was more than he ever wanted to experience. He leaned back and held Kima's worried face in his hands.

"I'm sorry for that. I guess I was having a nightmare," he admitted.

"You were having a nightmare and screaming my name? What was it about?" she asked.

"Your father kidnapping you to force you to marry

Nelson and me dying by his hands; or his foot rather. I couldn't get to you. They were taking you away and I couldn't get to you," Dayton explained while still trying to regain control of his breathing.

"Dayton? Listen to me," Kima said softly. "I'm right here with you. My father doesn't have me, you're not dying or dead and nothing or no one will come between us. We're together, right here in Bozeman at a hotel after flying hours to get here to safety. Yes, what could have happened didn't happen and it never will. I'm safe; you're safe and I love you. Come, lay with me," she coaxed.

Dayton wasn't sure he would be able to close his eyes and rest until he had them on the Sullivan Ranch. He knew he would have a lot to explain to his family, but he would do that after Nick and Parker's wedding. He hadn't planned on introducing Kima to his family like this. They won't be happy with the circumstances that had him and Kima fleeing Australia for their protection. What he did know is that his family would be supportive. They were already expecting him for the wedding, which was in a few days. For now, until he was ready to give answers for all that had happened, he and Kima would stay in each other's arms at the airport hotel. He may have had a nightmare, but for now, Oscar Tillery didn't have his hands on Kima. Dayton knew he would die before he let that happen.

As Kima lay back on the bed, Dayton laid his head on her chest as she tried to soothe him by rubbing his head and face. As she did so, he placed his hand over her belly where their child was and prayed that even at twenty-seven, he was ready to be a father. Anyone who came to take Kima and his child away from him had better be ready for the fight of their lives. He wouldn't go down easy. Had it only been two months since the drama all started? Dayton thought about that as he tried to go back to sleep or some semblance of it. He wouldn't get any real restful sleep until they were behind the gates of the Sullivan Ranch.

1

Two months ago
Sydney, Australia

Dayton Sullivan moved about as quietly as he could around the open living room area of the one-bedroom unit or flat in Sydney, Australia, which belonged to his girlfriend, Kima McDonald. He was thankful for the cream colored, plush shag carpet that covered the room and masked his footsteps. It wasn't easy for a man who stood at six-foot-four, two-hundred-and-twenty pounds to walk soundlessly. He was pretty much the exact height and weight of his favorite retired National Basketball Association, or NBA player, Dwyane Wade. The last thing he wanted to do was to wake her up after their all-night marathon lovemaking session. How either of them are still breathing after the level of acrobatics they took each other through, loving across most of the surfaces in the bedroom and not just the bed, still astounded him. It was definitely a result of how intense their love for each other has been since they first met over six months ago. In the United States, a place like this would be called an apartment. Dayton was still getting used to the various names of apartments based on the country he was in at any given time, traveling the world as a professional racecar driver.

Though he had every reason to still be asleep at this early morning hour, he was wide awake and about to do what he usually did a day following a win on the raceway like the one here in Sydney, Australia, called *TOBIT Motorsports*, one of the most popular ones in the world. He was packing up his latest medal, the *Barry Sheene Medal* for outstanding leadership, media interaction, character, personality, fan appeal and sportsmanship throughout the season.

The morning was quiet as he reached to the white marble and glass coffee table for the local newspaper where his face graced the cover yet again. Dayton was proud of himself. Though he doubted himself throughout his career, even now, at the age of twenty-six, his family back home on the Sullivan Ranch in Bozeman, Montana, always knew he would be a winner.

He is the youngest male of the Sullivan clan and yes, he was once again a winner. In his latest race, he came in first place, as was predicted by all news media outlets. This morning, the win from the day before felt different. He knew it the moment he crossed the finish line first in his latest, specially crafted *Formula E, Ferrari 1000 GP* electric car in his first ever electric-racing series. The race had been what the future is going to be in racing. Dayton knew that he'd just put on the show of his life, a career enhancing win. That's a lot for someone his age, height and weight. The usual was that race car drivers should be short in stature and small in weight so that the weight in the car is as light as possible to add to the speed that a driver could achieve. That was no longer the case. These days, it's more important that drivers focus on his strength, stamina, training and conditioning. He had to be in immaculate physical condition while also being at the top of the cognitive skills game to provide the best performance and control of his race car. Dayton had no doubt he was all of that. Racing was his life and so he was completely focused on it. The best part of racing was that he had the best team in place to be sure he didn't falter. Still, something was different in the light of day. He had a feeling it had a lot to do with the woman still asleep in the bed he hated getting out of. His restlessness would have woken her up, so he tiptoed out to have a moment of reflection on just how important racing still was to him. Being involved with Kima was changing his focus on what his priorities were. Was being on the track really the right track in life for him? He always thought it was and would continue to be, but now, he was beginning to see what his mother had always instilled in him, his three brothers and his sister; family and love was everything. He was starting to see that.

"Packing again, I see."

Dayton smiled without turning around. His hope of not waking Kima, the woman who had crept her way through every defense he'd set up to not get personally involved with any one woman, was out of the window. She was now up with him. He'd fought his attraction to her for over a year. Six months ago, they gave into the steamy glances and sexually enticed flirting game that led to their first incredible night together. What he thought would be his usual romp with a sexy woman turned into a full-fledged, yet secret relationship; a relationship he was all in for. The secret they had to keep about seeing each other was tearing him up inside.

Hearing Kima's sweet voice, Dayton turned from his kneeling position on the floor and slid onto the white leather sofa. His eyes rested on her standing in the bedroom doorway looking like a goddess; his goddess. All he saw was body, body, body everywhere from her perfectly toned legs, where she stood at five-foot-nine, to her flared hips and large breasts that threated to break free of the three snaps of her tank-top that held them in place. Oh, how he loved that resting place for his head. When she turned and quickly wiggled her ample, perfectly shaped behind at him, he winked letting her know that he appreciated all that was before him. Best of all, she was all his, just as much as he was all hers.

Splaying his arms across the back of the chair with his legs wide open and planted on the floor, Dayton knew what was coming next and Kima didn't disappoint. She rushed over, planted herself in the center of his lap, wrapped her arms around his neck with her knees on either side of him. Before any other words were spoken, she kissed him deeply; an action he welcomed as much as he welcomed his next breath. The kiss was fire-filled and potent as she covered his mouth with hers, moaning into his mouth when she took what she needed by slipping her tongue between his lips and searching for his tongue to begin mating with it. With his hands resting on her butt cheeks, which more than filled his large hands, he returned her eager fervor, decimating her mouth with his in the most passionate way. When his hands began moving up on the inside of her shirt, Kima pulled back and winked at him as he had done to her.

"If you keep those hands moving, there will be a repeat of last night, right here on this sofa. My legs are still quivering," Kima kidded and turned to the table to see what he had been doing.

"Don't you dare try to tempt me with even more of a good time!" Dayton quipped in return.

"Is that your latest medal?" Kima asked.

"No, that's the one from my win at the Monaco Formula One Grand Prix motor racing event held on the Circuit de Monaco back in May."

"To your mom?" she asked.

Dayton turned Kima's face back to him and smiled against her lips before raising his hands and sliding them through the thickness of her brown and gold curly flowing tresses.

"You know me so well. Yes, to my mom, along with the front-page article in the *Sydney Morning Herald*. This was an interview I actually liked. You know how I am about these kinds of showpieces."

"You don't enjoy the attention?" Kima said slyly. Dayton knew she was joking. You can't be a professional racecar driver and not love the attention from the media, and especially, the fans.

"I love the attention from you more than anything," he sighed against her face.

When Kima shifted around on him, Dayton chuckled. She had so much power over him.

"I can feel your attention under me," she whimpered with rising desire, nipping at his lips once again.

"If only there was time. You know there isn't. I shouldn't have stayed the night. All of this cloak and dagger, moving and shaking we're doing is getting the best of me. I hate that we have to sneak around like this. I'm twenty-seven, you're twenty-eight and we should be doing whatever we want to do with each other without having to hide any part of it."

When her head dropped, Dayton kicked himself for messing up the mood of the moment.

"This is all my fault. I can't believe I've allowed my father to control my life the way that he has. My mother warned me about letting my life get to this point. What can I say, he's my father," she asserted, before sliding from his lap to the spot next to him on the chair where she placed her feet against the edge of the cocktail table in front of them.

"Baby, I'm not placing any blame. I would rather have you like this than not have you at all, especially when you walk around in nothing but sexy panties and a white tank top. You turn me into a bumbling idiot who loves and lusts after you unconditionally."

Dayton snuggled her neck before kissing her there. He then leaned forward to return to packing as Kima picked up the newspaper and scanned the article.

"This story on you was a good one. Your latest win was a big one. An electric race car? Did you see my dad do a happy dance? You are the top driver on his team. You are why we have sold out crowds at every race."

Dayton turned to her.

"*Your* team. You own *TOBIT Motorsports* and the team. Your father has taken over, but you are still the owner, even though most of the day-to-day is run by the board. That's strictly for decision making, but let there be no mistake in you recognizing that you own the company. I get that Oscar Tillery, the snake that he is, is your father and *he's* controlling everything that was built by your grandfather and passed on to your mother, but in essence, you own it all; everything. I work for you, the sexiest boss I've ever known," he smiled and winked when she blushed.

"I know. *TOBIT Motorsports* is one of the top international raceways and has some of the best teams in the world. Because of your winning streak, our last five wins have been because of you. That doesn't even count the number of personal and individual wins you've racked up over the past three years that you've been a part of our team."

"I wish I could say I've enjoyed all of it, but I haven't. The last six-months have been the most amazing for more reasons than just racing."

Dayton blew a kiss her way and Kima acted like she caught it mid-air and placed it on the part of her body where she wanted it the most. When she chose one of her nipples which stood at attention through the thin material of her shirt, Dayton fanned himself. She knew how much he loved her breasts. Blowing kisses at each other was their thing. They did it when they were alone and picked really personal places on their bodies to place the imaginative kiss. In public, they picked a place that wouldn't draw too much attention to them like their lips, cheeks or arms.

"I love you too, my love," Kima acknowledged.

Dayton felt her hand caressing his bare back as her touch gave him chills.

"We should be able to love without hiding. The thought that, to your father and the rest of the racing circuit, you're set to marry this clown, Nelson Gaynor, who you don't love, eats the hell out of me every day. You don't even like him and you barely know him. Why would you let Oscar do this to you?" Dayton pleaded, and then stopped. He felt himself going on the attack because his hands were tied in the situation between

Kima and her father. Oscar may be the man who adopted her after marrying her mother, Hydea when she was a little girl, but the man he is today has earned little respect from her. He got that she still had the respect for him that she's always had, despite how much of a crook Oscar was turning out to be. He had the utmost respect for his own parents who were nothing like her father. David and Marta Sullivan loved all of their children. They would never ask any of them to compromise who they were for money; never.

"I don't know what to do, Day."

Dayton rubbed her leg when she called him by his nickname. He did so to reassure her that he wasn't blaming her. Despite his anger over it all, he loved her unconditionally.

"I love you and that's what's important," he said.

"You know I'm not going to marry Nelson. As much as I don't want to marry him, he doesn't want to marry me. Like you said, we don't even know each other. I met him a few times and we smiled at each other. Once over dinner with our fathers, we could see that they were trying to get us to hook up, but I wasn't interested. I fake painful cramps at the table. With them being all men, I saw their embarrassment when I started talking about my period. My dad shooed me away. I laughed all the way home," Kima laughed.

"This is some old school, forced marriage in order to merge the family money, type of situation. It's ridiculous. We already suspect that Oscar can see something has been going on between me and you. What will happen if he finds out? He will have to find out. There's no way I'm going to sit by and let you marry another man. It's never going to happen, Kima. The longer we put this off the crazier it will be."

Dayton felt himself getting angry and reigned his feelings in. Now wasn't the time. Not when they'd had a wonderful night together.

"I know, I know. I'm going to come up with something. I promise I will. Let's forget about that for now and focus on us and what we've found with each other. My father will not be supportive of how much we love each other, but your family sounds like they'll be different. Let me help you pack your medal to send home to your mother along with the newspaper article and then, let's talk about the day when I will get to meet them. Tell me again who everybody is."

Dayton kissed Kima's cheek as she moved closer, grabbed more paper to wrap the medal in while putting the stress of Oscar's latest antics in their rearview mirror; at least for the moment.

"Okay, there is my father, David Sullivan who runs the largest ranch in Bozeman with over 400,000 acres of land, with more added from recent purchases. The original purpose of the ranch was for the purpose of raising and feeding grazing livestock. My family has changed that with major plans for making a large section of the ranch family-friendly. There are huge event facilities on the property along with two major amusement parks, large summer camps facilities, hotels, family cabins, business parks and a lot more. Another large section is being developed for additional state of the art technology centers and business parks, all operated by solar energy. When I decided to go into racecar driving, my family built a large section up around auto maintenance, auto part buy and selling and a major plan where cars are built, especially the new electric cars."

"Like the one you raced yesterday?" she asked.

"Exactly like that one. The two that I have were built from scratch right on that part of the ranch. They get orders for cars pretty much on a weekly basis. The family owns it but it's run by a large subsidiary of the Sullivan Ranch. The ranch is divided into six major sections, with the most important section being the family ranch. That's a very private part of the ranch and no one can access it from any location without coming across hundreds of ranch hands who, anyone trying to sneak on the property, would not want to go up against. In all, the entire ranch employs over three thousand employees who either work for the businesses in one of the five other sections or who run the day-to-day of the family side with my mother and her large staff."

"Whew, that right there is a lot. I can't wait to see it all," she said.

"You will love it. Marta Sullivan is the true leader of all things Sullivan. My dad likes to think that he's in charge, but yeah, it's my mother. She is a *force*. We all jump when she speaks, especially when she means business. She likes to keep the family ranch as close to her as she can, so outside staff and visitors are limited and screened. My dad is CEO of all ranch activities, but my brothers, Perry and Shelton have total oversight and control of everything. My oldest brother is Perry. He's responsible for everything around ranch expansion including the portion of land that they're about to begin construction of a family friendly go-cart track."

"You told me about that. Are you still planning to have a professional race track built there? One that will be as large as the *Caraway Speedway* in North Carolina?"

Dayton was giddy at the idea that he could actually be part owner of his own raceway as well as owning his own team. So far, he's spent his entire career racing for others. He was ready to own.

When he first shared that idea with others, that's when his good working relationship ended with Oscar. The man had been banking on years and years of having his wins done by someone else. Dayton wanted to win under his own name; under the Sullivan name. His family was his biggest sponsors, but he could see taking that even further.

"Yes. I have a conference call with my brothers today. They're ready to show me the final draft plans for the track. Some construction has begun, but I want to see the final specs on the track itself."

"Nice. Okay, who's next?" Kima asked.

After Perry, there is Shelton. He is the financial brains behind everything that is the Sullivan Ranch. If it wasn't for him and his finance and technology acumen, who knows where the ranch would be. He has his PhD in finance and one in architecture. He is a beast when it comes to knowledge. Besides all that he does for the ranch, he has his own business which include a construction company, architectural firm and finance management firm. He oversees a large office park in downtown Bozeman with a staff of over three hundred. More about all of what he does later. We would be here all night all day if I tried to lay out how smart and business savvy he is."

"I need to meet him. I own a company and I know nothing about business. I think my father likes it that way. Who's next?" she asked.

Kima's words sounded glum. Dayton knew how she felt, but he also knew that wouldn't be for long. He was on board to help her find whatever it was she wanted to do with her life. Oscar didn't support any of her dreams, but he would.

"My brother Nick is a fire fighter. He's actually the captain of the largest firehouse in Bozeman. He's getting ready to marry Parker Wingate, one of the ranch veterinarians. I told you about the wedding coming up in two months, right after the Canada race. He's also a major stakeholder in all of the ranch expansion ideas."

"We're still going for the wedding, right? I get to meet your family?"

Dayton leaned over and quickly kissed her on the lips. He heard the unsurety in her voice.

"Baby, I wouldn't dare go home for the wedding and not take the time to introduce you to my family. I've been pretty closed mouth about us out of caution. By then, I'm hoping we'll have all of this mess with Oscar settled and we won't have to creep around anymore."

"I'm excited to meet them. So, Nick, he was the one working in New York until the accident you told me about?"

"Right. He was fighting a fire in New York and he could have been killed. He was severely injured and a fireman actually died. My family practically dragged him back to the ranch to recuperate and he decided to make his life there, especially after meeting Parker."

Kima chuckled.

"I remember you told me that your mother gave your father and brother an ultimatum when they went to New York after finding out about the accident; something Nick didn't even call to tell your family about."

"Trust me. No one messes with Marta Sullivan; no one. Nick tried it. When my father and Perry went to check on him, my mother told my father that he and Perry should not come back home if Nick wasn't with him."

Kima laughed out loud. Hearing about the antics of his mother had her missing her own mother. She missed having that little bit of family that she did have. Now, all she had was Oscar. She was learning more and more about him that she didn't like with each passing day.

"She wasn't serious, was she?"

"Oh, yes, she was and my father knew it. Nick returned to the ranch without question. He knew better. My mother hates to fly, but she would have if he didn't come home. You do whatever my mother says or there will be hell to pay. We all learned that growing up."

"I'm next in line and behind me, pulling up the rear is my sister, Brielle, the baby of the family. She oversees every event on the ranch. One of the six sections is dedicated to family enjoyment. There has been so much construction on that side that in the next few years, it will mirror *Disney World*. I still can't believe the hundreds of thousands of visitors the ranch gets each year and even with all of the event space available, there is still a long waiting list to get in. A lot of companies hold retreats and conferences on the ranch, too. There is a major banquet and several conference facilities."

"So, you're the only one not in Bozeman."

Dayton didn't want to get into his reasons for needing to get away from ranch life. That feeling that kept him up the night before resurfaced.

With the box ready to send to his mother, he stood and stretched.

"Yes, I'm the only one. It's getting late Kima. I should go. In the daylight, the media will spot me in a second and that's the last thing we need."

"I know. I'm sorry we have to do this, but I promise, it's only temporary. I'll think of something."

Dayton turned and pulled her into his arms.

"No, we'll think of something. Just not today. I want to get to the track and check on the car."

"You mean get on the track. I know you're itching to get behind the wheel without having to worry about racing."

"Baby, I'm not much if I'm not behind the wheel of a car."

"To me, you're everything. Don't forget to drop this box off to your mother today. The last time, you forgot and it sat around for weeks. What does your mother do with all of the medals and trophies you send home?"

"We all have our own houses on the ranch. Though I'm hardly ever in mine, my mother keeps a room in my house where she's created trophy shelves and medal boxes. It's her way of staying close to me when I'm not home. I miss her. I miss everyone, but especially her."

"You'll see her soon."

"So will you. Shall we eat breakfast before I leave?"

"Or..." Kima said and winked.

"I would but a quickie is not in my plans for this morning. I want to be able to love you for hours, and hours and hours," he quipped.

"*Mmm*, my favorite song describing my favorite thing."

"Mine, too, but we need to watch the time. I need to be able to slip out of here without being seen. Now, food?" he asked again.

Before she could respond, Kima's body stiffened when she glanced out of the window of her flat and saw her father's jeep pull up across the street.

"Oh, my goodness! What is he doing here at this hour?"

Dayton turned and got the shock of his life. He too saw Oscar's truck pull up into a parking space.

"Why, why, why?" Kima asked as she moved around aimlessly trying to figure out what to do.

"Who knows. He's a live-wire," Dayton admitted.

"He usually has a driver escort him around in his limo or big trucks with the blacked-out windows. If he's driving himself, he's up to something."

Dayton didn't wait for an answer. He raced into the bedroom and threw on his clothes as quickly as he could, carrying his brown leather, steel-toed cowboy boots in his hand. He may be out of Bozeman, but the cowboy in him was wherever he went.

"Baby, I have to get out of here."

"Take the stairs. You know my father would never hike up six flights of stairs for any reason. Where did you park?" she asked.

"About eight blocks away. I wasn't taking any

chances."

Grabbing the box and looking to be sure there were no signs of Oscar anywhere, Dayton stole one last, quick kiss and peered out of her door before moving to the stairwell right next to her flat at the end of the hallway. He waited until Kima's door closed before he let out the breath he'd been holding. If she hadn't spotted Oscar's car out of the window, he would have surprised them and possibly caught them together. Dayton felt like that teenager back on the ranch when he would sneak girls on the ranch and risked getting caught when he needed to sneak them off; something he learned to become an expert at after watching his brothers do it for years.

Realizing he put his jacket on without his shirt, which was still in his hands, he took a few seconds to remedy that by changing. While doing so, he heard the elevator door open as loud footsteps made their way to Kima's door. Dayton stood along the white concrete wall, waiting to make his exit after Oscar was inside. The metal steps would surely make noise under his feet. He was in a bind and it would be worse if Oscar spotted him. Not taking a chance, he waited before he moved.

2

Oscar waited before he knocked on Kima's door. He knew she was hiding something and probably someone in her flat. She wouldn't know that he didn't just show up this morning by happenstance, but he'd driven by the night before, after another successful race at their raceway. He would soon be headed out of the country on another trip to South America. He would soon have to start answering for all of the crooked deals he's been making lately. He also had no doubt that the board of their company would discover that he has a person inside who ran the finance department who has been helping him to embezzle money; actions that would soon come to light. He had to get Kima onboard with what he has planned for her that would yield him the money he would need to get out from under the boulders of debt he was in.

Hoping to surprise her and who he knew would be inside, he knocked hard and waited. Oscar leaned his ear against the door to see if he could hear any movement of people shuffling around. There was no need for her to hide things with Dayton from him any longer. Now that he was about to catch them, he could get it all out in the open and tell Dayton he needed to walk away. Their play time was about to come to an end.

Just then the door opened and Kima stood on the other side in a large, fluffy pink robe pulled tight around her. Her hair was all over the place as if she'd just rolled out of bed.

"Daddy, what are you doing here this early in the morning?" she asked, closing the door behind them.

Dayton couldn't resist. Even though he was in the stairwell, he hadn't moved. Now, curiosity was getting the best of him. He too wanted to know what was the cause of Oscar's early morning arrival. He opened the exit door as quietly as he could and crouched near Kima's door to listen in, hoping that no one would come out of their unit and catch him looking like a prowler.

"I was out driving and I wanted to talk to you. I want to know why you and Nelson haven't set a wedding date yet. His father, Andrew is one of my closest business partners. He called me late last night to say that Nelson has been trying to reach you and you haven't been responding. You know what this means to me and to you."

"Daddy, you are trying to force me to marry a man I don't love. That's crazy, even for you. This isn't nineteen hundred."

"Don't smart talk me! I know what year it is. This

is a business deal that has to take place. Besides, Nelson is a great kid. He just graduated law school and has joined one of the most prestigious firms in the United States. His father owns one of the largest raceways in the country, in North Carolina. Merging our two companies together will be a massive financial windfall for us. We're struggling, Kima. I told you that."

Oscar kept to himself that what he'd just told her was a lie. Thankfully, she wouldn't know because she had no real interest in the company left to her by her mother.

"We're struggling because you have messed up the money. I don't understand that and that's my own fault for not being involved in more of the business."

"You don't have to. I have it all covered. Our racing teams have been very successful. That may change now that Dayton wants to do his own thing. I haven't been successful in convincing him that he needs to continue with us. I've thrown more money at him and more power, but nothing has worked. I guess it's because he has his own money through his family. I didn't know until recently that his family was so well off. I need this deal with the Gaynor family if I'm going to keep our business running. We need the money," he pleaded.

"No, you need the money. I don't care about any of this. I only care that mommy's legacy is dwindling because of mismanagement."

"What are you trying to say? Are you saying that I've mismanaged things? There is a board, you know.

It's not just me. I could be them too."

"Who else? You took control after mommy died and it's gone downhill ever since. She didn't want this to happen."

"Is that why you've been going through her things? I heard you were at the house looking through boxes of your mother's things. There is nothing there. I told you what your mother's wishes were for you and the business. She would want you to do this for me; to help me get us out of the red. I expect you to honor me as your father and do this. You call Nelson today and plan out the announcement of your engagement and come up with a wedding date. I want it done today. It may be better to just get married at the courthouse or by a priest right here in Australia."

"What? No way. This is insane. I can't handle this right now. I will not be browbeaten into a marriage with some random guy for money's sake. I bet mommy is turning over in her grave at what you're trying to do."

"Really? You want to take it there? I don't think you want to. Your mother is gone and that's that. I am your father, the only family you have and you will do this or you'll find yourself alone."

Kima was about to respond when watching Oscar start sniffing around her flat bothered her. He was literally taking in large whiffs of air like a bloodhound dog.

"What are you doing?" she asked.

"I think I smell a man's cologne. It's light, but I

smell it. Do you have someone here? Is there a man here?" Oscar demanded as he moved away from the door and roamed the open area.

"What business is it of yours? I'm a grown woman. If I want to have a man in my own place, I will. For your benefit and to get you moving to your next destination, there is no man here. I don't know what you think you smell, but there's nothing and no one here."

"You're lying. My business or not, you're being really sneaky these days. You hardly come by the house anymore. You run off after every race now, not to mention your sudden interest in being at every race for the past year. This year, you have traveled all over the world following our races; something you have never done before. What gives? Is there a reason? Is there a person you're following and not just the circuit?"

Kima watched her father cross his arms across his large belly, barely able to make his hands meet. The buttons on his white shirt had seen better days of trying to stay connected. She already knew that he never wore his suits buttoned up because his beer gut wouldn't allow it. If she didn't know any better, she would say that he was still in the suit he'd had on the night before. Had he not been home?

"I'm like the races, that's all. It's interesting to see. You used to complain that I never sat in the owner's box. Now that I do, you still complain."

"Hmm. I'll take that for now, but I sense that's a lie too."

"Why are you really here? You could have called me on the phone to lay me out about Nelson like you tend to do just about every single day."

"You're being unwavering and I don't like it. What's really going on with you?"

Kima needed to change his focus.

"Have you been out all night? I know that's what you had on last night. Did you get up and put the same clothes back on? What? Are you seeing someone? You're always wondering about my personal life. I hear the stories about you and many much younger women, some younger than me."

"My life is none of your business. I'm *your* father. I get to ask you about your life, while you don't get the same privilege."

Kima was going for the kill. This, she knew would have him running for the exit.

"You know, there is some talk going around about you and the Snyder girl. Isn't she like, nineteen? I was planning on asking her out to lunch one day soon. I think I'll do that today. I wonder what we'll talk about? She walked up to me yesterday at the race and said she had something she wanted to talk to me about. I saw her cut her eyes at you. Isn't her mother on the board? I have some time today. What do you think? Are we done here?" she asked.

Kima wanted to gloat openly, but held it in. With Oscar's pale skin, he was turning red as a beet. She still didn't know what her mother saw in him. He was flustered and turning left and right not knowing what to do.

Game, set, match, she thought.

Dayton heard the conversation and fumed so hot, he felt like his head was going to explode. He stood so fast that his car keys fell out of his grip to the floor. There was no way they wouldn't hear that sound. Rushing, he moved to the door and raced down the steps. Even as he did so, he could hear Oscar's footsteps in the hall just before he opened the door to the stairwell.

"Who was here?" Oscar asked Kima, now that they were in the hallway.

"What? How would I know. There are many units here. That could have been anyone."

Dayton stood still against the wall until he heard the door close and Oscar and Kima moved back into her unit.

With the speed he was glad he could muster up from being in shape, Dayton took the remaining steps two and three at a time until he reached the ground floor. Rather than exit on Kima's side of the building, he raced around two additional hallways until he reached the back of the building. Checking his surroundings, he darted and raced away from her building as fast as he could, pulling his hat out of his jacket pocket, place it on his head, far enough down to hide his face and he made his way to his waiting car. He vowed that this would be the last time he would play this game with Kima and her father. He loved her and wanted to be with her. It was time Oscar knew the truth. He had to be told that his plans for Kima to marry someone else was never going to happen. If it did, Dayton knew it would be over his own dead body.

3

Being in his 1966 Pontiac GTO, one of his favorite racing cars, Dayton felt at home, more than any other place. The track in Australia was one of his favorites. The idea of being able to drive two hundred miles an hour, legally, was enough to have him practically living on the track. He walked around his car, preparing for a practice session while he had the track to himself for the next hour. He needed to feel the speed under his feet while in his car in order to forget about the conversation between Kima and her father earlier in the day. The whole situation was unsettling. He loved how Kima handled it like a boss. Still, he needed to find a way to get them from under Oscar's foot.

Suited up, he watched as a member of his pit crew, Paul, guided others as they moved his car into position. He had already done ten laps with his baby, his, 1970 Dodge Charger R/T, the car that when he raced it at its top speed, he felt like the Vin Diesel's character, Dominic Toretto from the Fast and the Furious saga.

"Are you planning to slow your speed since you're not in a battle for first place of anything today?"

Dayton turned to find Rusty, his manager, coming down from the stands.

Dayton grinned as he slipped on his fire proof gloves, a requirement for being on the track and in any car.

"I was wondering if you were going to show up to watch me practice today. I assumed you would be on your way home to Los Angeles to see your family. I know your wife and kids are missing you with all of the back-to-back races we've had over the past three months. We have about eight weeks before the next race here followed by the big one in Canada. Surely, you're not going to hang around Australia until then."

"Is that thinking because you, yourself, are heading off for a secret rendezvous? Where to this time?" Rusty asked.

Dayton could never pull anything over on Rusty, the man who knew him better than anyone else on the racing circuit. Rusty had been his manager, personally picked by his father and brothers when he decided to go professional. His family wanted the best in the business and that's what they got in Rusty and his team. In fact, to this day, Rusty's high six-figure salary is paid by his family along with the salaries of the men who make up security and all-around get it done guys who are employed by Rusty. His mother insisted on having a guarantee that someone would have his interest and safety, and only his, in mind. Rusty also knew something that his family did not know; he knew about Kima.

As of this day, he's kept his family and his closest friends in the dark regarding his relationship with Kima, but not Rusty. He was the only person who knew that he'd fallen in love with her. He was the only person Dayton trusted while they were out on the road. Rusty knew the plans Oscar had for Kima, too. He also knew that there was no way that any of it was going to take place.

"Paris. I'm taking her to Paris for a week of romance, fine dining and relaxation."

"Still, Oscar doesn't know?" Rusty asked as he moved to lean against the car with the Sullivan written in large white letters on it.

"I don't care if he does or not. If so, he hasn't said anything or Kima would have told me."

"When I talked to you while you were driving here today, you said you thought he may have seen you at Kima's place last night?"

"There's more that I haven't told you. I haven't even told Kima because I don't want her to worry."

Rusty exhaled, something Dayton was prepared for.

"Do I need to sit for this? You know I'm all for having a good time and even being in love. Hell, I've been married for ten years. Being on the road with you and away from my family, I am still as much in love with my wife today as I was the moment I met her. I've watched you these past couple of years when you first went pro. I've seen a lot of women come and go, and there have been a lot of them. I keep telling you that you should own stock in a condom company. You once claimed that you would never fall in love because the track was your one and only love. You also claimed to enjoy many women, but not love any and that's with a mutual understanding that you make with them all. Those Sullivan brothers of yours set a crazy example when it comes to your non-stop sex life, but I'll stay out of that. I thought you were never, ever going to let feelings invade your prowess. I see things have changed."

"You know me so well. I didn't set out to fall in love with Kima, but I did. It took no time at all."

"What is it that I need to prepare myself for? I already know you love her."

"Last night – I saw Oscar outside of her building. He knows I was there."

"How?"

"I've suspected for about a week before last night, but I wasn't sure. Then last night happened and I knew; I knew that he'd been following her. He would know that she comes to my hotel all the time and doesn't leave until the morning. Sometimes, she stays over for days."

"The man is a chameleon," Rusty noted, crossing his legs at the ankles, while kicking up dirt with this large brown Timberland boots.

"Kima was asleep. I got up to look over some emails

my brothers sent me. I grabbed a beer, leaned against the window and looked out only to see his car parked two blocks from her building, but close enough that he could see me as well as I could see him. He was parked under a light, so his face was clear. I acted like I didn't see him and moved away from the window. That wasn't the first time that I thought I saw him creeping around. That was the first time we sort of locked eyes."

"Then he shows up this morning?" Rusty asked.

Dayton nodded. The moment he reached his car after sneaking out of Kima's building, he called Rusty to let him know what happened. He told him he'd be at the track if he wanted to stop by. Rusty was handling some business and wasn't sure he'd make it before the practice session was over, but Dayton had an inkling he would. Rusty was nothing if he wasn't someone that could be counted on; someone dependable.

"I should have left before this morning. I didn't think he'd actually come to her flat, though. I didn't tell Kima when he surprised her. I acted surprised along with her. Even though I snuck out, like some teenager, pissed that I still have to, I listened to them talk through the door. He's still forcing her to marry this Nelson guy. This is the wildest thing I have ever heard about in this day and time."

"Yeah, well, men like Oscar don't die, they multiply year after year. Look at the evilness that runs our country now? People think that an evil mentality will die off with a certain person, but it doesn't. What finally happened?"

"Stupid me, I dropped my keys and they clanged to the tiled floor outside of her door. I raced like a bat out of hell before he caught me. I wouldn't really care if he did if it wasn't Kima I was thinking about."

"What do you know about him? I mean, what do you know about how he came into her life and her mother's?"

"I don't know the full story. Kima and I talk bits and pieces about it here and there. Kima was born in Brazil where her mother grew up. Sometime before that, her mother's mother met Kima's grandfather, Eli Tobit, who was the original owner of TOBIT Motorsports. At that time, he was married to someone else but got Kima's grandmother pregnant. Because of his life in America with his family, he never claimed Hydea as his own and pretty much abandoned them."

"Damn, that's sad," Rusty said with remorse for a woman he never knew.

"I know, right? I would never abandon my child for any reason. Anyway, Eli, his wife and their only son were killed a plane crash while flying at night into Martha's Vineyard, Massachusetts."

"Wait, isn't that where John Kennedy, Jr. was going when he crashed?"

"One in the same. Crazy, right?"

"It seems, secretly, Eli had written Hydea into his will if anything should happen to him. By now, she was an adult, around twenty. With his wife and son dying in the same crash, that left everything he had to Hydea, including the motorsport company. She knew nothing about racing or business. She was a young woman living in Brazil who then found herself pregnant. Kima doesn't know what happened to her father. She only remembers Oscar, who at that time, worked for Hydea's father at the company. He somehow weaseled his way into Kima's mother's life and bam, four or five years later, they were married. He was like thirty-five or so at that time. Her mother was still pretty young. A board had already been in place, though Hydea owned the company. When Kima's mother died, mysteriously, some years ago, she had left everything to Kima, to Oscar's surprise. He thought he had the last version of her will, but her mother had changed it without telling him."

"Man, this stuff is movie worthy."

"It is and now, Kima is caught up. You know she believes Oscar may have killed her mother. That's another whole story. It's also why I have to get her away from him. For now, I'll settle for a week with her in Paris. After that, I don't know."

"Look, I know you want to protect Kima. I get that. You are going to need more than just you to do that. Have you thought of reaching out to your family for support? I don't have to tell you that you have the greatest family on this side of the Jordan. They would kill for each other."

Dayton knew that. He was planning on looping his

brothers in on what was going on. He wanted them all to meet Kima. He wasn't sure of what that perfect time would look like; at least not yet.

"I'm planning on it. I spoke to my mother a week ago and she asked about you, Lori and your kids. She's wondering when you're coming back to the ranch. You should see the amusement park. It wasn't there the last time you were there. Your kids are bigger now, so they'll really appreciate all the rides and games."

"I'll have to do that. First, my priority is your races. Go ahead and get on the track. I missed you practicing in the first car I saw them pulling away before bringing this one out. This is your favorite, I know. Have you decided which one you're racing in Canada?"

"I think this one. I'll have to have it shipped, but yeah, this one."

"Okay, kid. Let me see what you got," Rusty exclaimed.

Dayton signaled to his crew who hustled over to help him with his helmet, check his gear and aid him with getting in the car. Getting inside was through the window only. He still loved that about racing.

Giving Rusty and his team the thumbs up that he was ready, Dayton took off slow at first, but once he hit the track, he pushed a button where rap music from Tupac would flood the car, helping to keep him focused. He had to turn his thoughts away from Kima and her father, remembering it was always safety first on the track and that meant concentrating.

As his speed climbed from eighty, to one-twenty, to one-fifty, he pushed the car even further as it headed toward two-hundred, even when he took to the inside of the track. This was it. This is what he woke up every day to get to. This was the right track.

4

Paris, France

Exiting what Kima would call a spa and not just a bathroom in the suite she and Dayton were staying in, she paused in the doorway after an hour spent luxuriating in the sexiest looking marble and gold clawfoot tub she'd ever been in. She made note to look into having one installed in her place back at home.

The Four Seasons Hotel George V, in Paris, France was a dream she never knew she needed in her life. Looking around the extra-large bedroom with its dark redwood furniture, including the four-poster bed, covered in D. Porthault Jours De Paris sheets, the second most expensive in the world at around nineteen hundred dollars, Kima didn't know how she'd get so lucky as to have a man who knew about the finer things in life. Splurging like this wasn't a priority for either of them, but there was one thing about Dayton; he loved to spoil her. She was amazed that while she was taking a much-needed bath, Dayton had lit flameless candles all around their room setting the stimulatingly, romantic scene. She loved that they could go from having a romantic atmosphere like this one to love in while also taking advantage of clawing at each other in a tiny closet. No matter the time or place, they loved getting in that good, good!

Standing in only a white plush robe with a matching towel wrapped snug around her semi-wet hair, Dayton looked over at her from his vantage point on one side of their king-sized bed with an intense stair that made her shiver. In her twenty-eight years, no man has ever looked at her the way he does. She had been known to favor dating older men, finding more in common with them, but when Dayton first looked at her over a year ago, there was something in his eyes that told her, despite him being a year younger than her, she needed and wanted to know more about the popular racecar driver. Six months after that, it happened.

Seeing Dayton shirtless, sitting up in bed with his legs crossed at the ankles, he looked more handsome and virile than she'd ever seen him before. He once told her he was an old soul, something he'd been told all of his life by those closest to him. Today, there was nothing old looking about him. He was ripe and prime and he was all hers. Clad only in black boxer briefs and a big, bright amorous smile, Kima leaned against the doorway and returned his smile.

"Candles? Where did you find candles? The room looks amazing. The dead of night, pitch black outside, enticing and inviting inside," she noted.

"Enticing and inviting? I have achieved my goal," Dayton gloried, crossing his arms across his broad, muscled chest.

"Yes, you have if that's what you were going for. This hotel, this suite it's all remarkable. How did you pick this place? You continue to astonish me with how romantic you can be."

"I'm sure I do. You once told me that you liked dating older men because they had already learned a thing or two about romance, something you love. I would say good for them, but I won't. It's actually good for me because whatever it is they thought they were doing, they clearly weren't doing it right enough to hold your attention because here we are – you and me. You are so beautiful."

Kima blushed as she looked bashfully away. Dayton made her feel all mushy inside. Everything about her loved him. She wondered if it was too soon in their relationship for her to tell him that she was in love with him. Sure, they would toss out the love word to each other, but saying I love you and being in love weren't the same in her book. She was madly in love with Dayton.

"The hotel? How did you decide on this one? It's so elegant and quixotic and the view from the many windows is unbelievable. I could stare out all day and night. I love it here."

"Baby, I would love to take the credit for picking this hotel, but I can't. I called my sister and told her that I was going to be spending a week with the most incredible woman I've ever met. She knew that meant that I wanted only the best."

"Ah, Brielle hooked us up."

Dayton had told her some things about his family and she was looking forward to learning more.

"Yes."

"Your family knows about me?"

Kima wasn't sure of how far things with her and Dayton were going to go, but she was hoping for something long-term; possibly forever. She knew his family meant the world to him and she wanted to know them.

"Just my sister, for now. If I told my mother about you right now, she'd be threatening my life if I didn't bring you home to the Sullivan Ranch for her to meet you."

"But you told your sister?"

Kima moved away from the wall as she took the towel down from her hair and attempted to soak more of the water out of it after she stepped briefly into the shower after her bath in order to wash her hair.

"I tell Brielle everything. She and I are the closest of my siblings. Let me correct that; we're all pretty close, but Brielle and me being the youngest, we have a special bond. Of course, she wanted to know everything about you. I promised her I would fill her in, but at that time, I needed her to book a nice place for us to stay in. She knows everything about the best places to stay around the world. We get people and companies on the ranch all the time, so she stays up on where they're coming from and the kind of arrangements available in other cities and countries."

"The ranch has this kind of place where people can stay?"

"Yes. It depends on the experience. Most of what we have are cabins for accommodations because it is a ranch. We have some that are high-end like this hotel suite and we also have them at the other end of the spectrum that gives a visitor the full living off the grid type of rustic cabin. There are over eighty cabins in all along with six hotels. At twenty-five, Brielle is amazing with all that she has accomplished. The look and feel of events and the cabins and everything else, even some of our own personal houses, is all her."

"You have a house on the ranch? You're never there? When do you ever go home?"

Kima gasped with delight when Dayton swung his long, perfectly toned legs around and placed his feet on the floor, his eyes still focused on her. He looked good. He smelled good. He was, what she now knew was, the perfect man.

When her gazed lowered to the large bulge prominently displayed between his legs, she knew she was in for a night of the most magical lovemaking a woman could experience. She was more than ready. Without thinking about what she was doing, Kima was too late to stop her tongue from venturing out of her mouth as she ceremoniously licked her lips, unable to contain her animalistic craving for him.

"I saw that," Dayton chuckled.

Kima laughed so hard that her robe gaped open, exposing her nakedness underneath.

"I didn't mean for you to see that," she quipped.

"What about that? Did you mean for me to see that?"

Kima watched Dayton's gaze darken to a sensual, erotic look. The way he looks at her never lies when it comes to how much he always wants her.

"Yes and no. I need lotion on first before you see all of this. I was in that tub soaking so long that only the most moisturizing lotion can do this skin any justice."

"Let me do that for you. Come here," Dayton signaled to her with his words and with a nod of his head. Like a moth to a flame, Kima moved quickly to stand before him, dropping the towel to the floor and leaving her robe open for his perusal.

"I'm glad you thought of this getaway. We needed this. Things are getting crazy with my father. I still don't know what I'm going to do."

The worry in her voice was evident. The moment she spoke of her father, Dayton's body stiffened, and not in a good way. She knew that he was thinking about the same thing that she was thinking.

"Kima, you are not marrying another man. I know I can't control you and your decision making, but what we share, it would kill me if I have to imagine that

Nelson guy touching you. My temper wouldn't be able to just live with that. I don't care what Oscar has gotten himself into, you marrying someone to merge families for money's sake is preposterous. You deserve better than that. I can't entertain that happening."

Dayton lowered his head and Kima pulled him close to her body as his hands slipped inside of the robe. He moved his fingers to lock behind her body, holding her to him.

"I wouldn't do that to you or me. No, I'm not marrying Nelson, not even for my father. Before I flew here to meet you this morning, I stopped by his house because I knew he was in South America. He's got something illegal going on and it involves weapons and drugs coming out of Colombia. He's been back and forth for a few months now and has been secretive about it. While at the house, I went through some of my mother's things and I found a bunch of papers. Inside at the very bottom of one box was a letter to me from her that I've never seen. I don't know how Oscar got it, but he never gave it to me. In it, she tells me how much she loves me and how sorry she was that she ever introduced Oscar into our lives, especially mine. She spoke about some of the illegal things he was involved in and warned me to be careful. She said things were going to be really tricky soon because she had obtained counsel to see to it that Oscar didn't get his hands on anymore of our money. She had found out some things and was planning on going to the authorities. There was a lot more in the letter, but I had to rush. I knew his housekeeper would be back to the house soon after I watched her leave for the store. I love Edna and wouldn't want her to have to choose sides. She goes the same time on the same day every week. I put the letter back in the box and grabbed the entire thing along with some other papers I saw and I hightailed it out of there."

Dayton leaned back and looked up at her, his eyes wide with fear.

"What if Oscar finds out you took that box? He has to know what's in it."

"That stuff had so much dust on it. I don't think he's even thought about any of it since my mother died two years ago. I was warned by my mother's attorney that it's possible my life was in danger. He believed Oscar had something to do with my mother's death; remember, I mentioned that to you before. He said there was a cover-up and that my mother's car was rigged to have the breaks fail when she crashed and it exploded, killing her instantly. I was too wracked with grief to even think about that."

"Maybe he can help you figure out what Oscar is really up to when it comes to your money. His bottom line in marrying you off is to first, get his hands on the rest of your money and then to combine your company with Andrew Gaynor's circuit and raceway out of North Carolina, one of the largest in the United States and in that state. Everyone knows Nelson and his father are crooks."

Kima could feel tears welling up in her eyes.

"We can't. That was Donald Weatherly. I thought I told you this but, he died, mysteriously four months after my mother died. He was in the midst of filing some papers based on my mother's wishes and he supposedly died from some boating accident that has yet to be investigated as a murder but instead, as an accidental fall overboard. His body was never found. There were rumors that he was pushed over while strapped to cinder blocks or something else that would prevent his body from rising again."

"Baby! You never told me any of this. How dangerous is Oscar and this Gaynor family? Are you in any danger? If Oscar can't get his hands on the big chunk of your money, would he harm you?"

Kima had the same fear but she didn't want Dayton to worry about her. She remembered times when her mother was deathly afraid of Oscar but was too afraid to leave him. Being forced to marry a man she didn't love was his latest scheme. She went along with the idea of it only to give her some time to think of what to do to get out of it. Even if she hadn't fallen in love with Dayton the day that they'd gone out on their first date, she was still never going to marry Nelson.

"I don't think so. I think any more mysterious happenings would raise even more red flags." Kima reached her hands up and cupped Dayton's face in her hands. "No more talk of my father or Nelson or anything else that isn't about me and you. You went through a lot to plan this week away for us and I don't want it wasted on anything but us. I want to make the most of our time," she said with obvious, sensual undertones.

Moving her robe to the side on either side of her body without removing it, Kima made her intentions very clear. She also knew that Dayton was more than willing to oblige her.

5

Dayton's eyes flared with awareness of the beautiful woman standing before him. He had planned this time away, not to focus on any drama, but to make sure, with his busy schedule, that he took the much-needed time to show Kima how he felt about her; how much he loved her. They both knew his past with women; there was never a time that there was only one. There were names and faces he could barely remember. That was the result of enjoying the pleasantries of intimacy without having to hang around for relationship-type behavior. That is, until he met Kima. At first, there was lust. Then that was followed-up, almost immediately with a level of affection that warranted having Kima for more than just the best sex of his life. He wanted more of his life to include her. This trip was their time away from the rat-race that was professional racecar driving and he wasn't going to let anything interrupt that.

He leaned forward and placed a kiss in the spot between her large breasts, which sat high on her chest, calling his name like a moth to a flame. With her, he didn't mind a little fire.

Kima watched the fiery glow in Dayton's eyes light up even more when she took his hands and placed them square on her breasts to add to the salacious way he was kissing her there. She wanted no doubt in the atmosphere of what she was talking about when she told him their trip away together would be magical. Being together wasn't always about sex, but for tonight, that's all she wanted them to focus on. There was always plenty of time for other kinds of fun. The things that kept their affair alive was how they enjoyed being together out of bed as much as they did in one.

When he gave her soft globes a light squeeze before pinching her nipples just the way she loved, Kima threw her head back and smiled, sucking a deep breath into her mouth, holding it for a few seconds to make sure she was able to focus on feeling and not breathing.

"Mmm, I have a lot I want to get into with you while we're here, but first, lotion?" he asked.

Kima winked at him with one eye.

"Um?" she jested.

Dayton cried out in laughter.

"None of that right now. I can give you a show for your eyes a little later. This is for you saying you needed to be covered in lotion," he laughed more.

Kima pointed to her suitcase but before she could move to get it, Dayton pulled her back in close to him, kissed her breasts again with the pad of his tongue, leaving a wet trail across them. When he blew on that trail, Kima's legs buckled, almost sending her to the floor if it were not for him holding her in place.

"I'm all yours," she uttered.

"Like I like it too. On the bed, on your stomach," he growled sexily.

With unwavering delight, Kima didn't question his request. She dropped her robe, being long past any modesty with the number of times he'd already seen her naked. The man had a sexual appetite that she was still getting used to, but very much loved.

Lying flat, her body surged with desire when she felt Dayton's presence above her, straddling her body with both knees on either side of her behind. When his hands made contact with her shoulders as he spread lotion across them, Kima closed her eyes and enjoyed the feel of his rough, yet tender touch. Her body was already on the verge of exploding with the way he was slowly caressing her skin. He moisturized her neck, then her full arms before taking his time on her back and sides. She fought the eager urge to squirm around underneath of him.

"How's that?" he whispered close to her ear.

"Ah, perfect. You have wonderful hands, along with other wonderful things," she asserted.

"Like *this*?" Dayton asked.

Kima felt his *this* immediately, snug, long and hard between the cheeks of her butt. She tried to reach back to touch any part of him, but Dayton swiped her hand away.

"Tease!" she declared, causing him to laugh out loud.

When he leaned down, close to her ear again, Kima quivered when the heat of his breath caressed her everywhere.

"Teasing makes it more erotic, don't you think?" he asked.

Before she could respond, the feel of Dayton's tongue fondling her ear before he sucked the lobe into his mouth and massaged it with his tongue had Kima clinching her fingers before grabbing onto the soft, plush fabric of the expensive cream, silk comforter.

"More!" she moaned out and found herself practically begging.

"There is a *lot* more," he replied.

Dayton slid further down her body. Kima felt the squirts of the lotion he applied to her behind and her mind reeled with so much desire that she tried with her might to turn over.

"I need to see you," she pleaded when he continued to hold out on her.

"In a minute. Let me finish giving the proper attention to this plump, round ass of yours. You know how much I love having my hands all over you."

"I know, but I need you, please? We have a whole week to go nice and slow. I get it. Before we got here today, I hadn't seen you in over a week and I'm overdue."

Kima wiggled a little more with the sensual way Dayton was caressing her. The moment his fingers slid between her legs and parted her womanly folds which were already dripping wet with the essence of her desire for him, she practically bucked up off of the bed. Kima held her teeth close together as her head moved from side to side when Dayton slid first one finger and then a second into her body from behind. When his lips caressed her butt and he lightly nibbled from one side to the other, Kima could feel her body about to explode. Dayton's magical fingers were working their magic on her.

Kima opened her legs slightly to give him more room as the suite filled with the sounds of her moans of pleasure.

"Ready for me, I see," Dayton said against her behind.

Kima couldn't get even a single word out as he lifted her hips so that her body was raised up just enough for him to place his head between her legs where she felt his tongue join his happy fingers in their pursuit to drive her wild with need.

With the comforter tight in her grip, Kima widened her legs even more and moved her body toward his mouth. Dayton lapped at her again and again as she responded to his titillating, pleasure-filled assault on her body.

Dayton fed from her like a starving man as the pad of his tongue provided the right amount of pressure on the hard nub of her pleasure principle that she knew greeted him with open arms.

As her hips moved in a circular motion, Dayton held onto her with his hands. She could feel the smile on his face knowing he never needed an eternity to get her to the point where she would soon be whistling at the moon. The moment was now, as her eyes clamped shut and her body roared as she gave into the craving. Her body fiercely quaked with an orgasm that had her losing control of her own body. If it had not been for Dayton holding her tight, she would have flopped right onto the floor.

Kima's screams of satiated joy pierced the quiet of the night. Knowing she couldn't help herself; she didn't care. Her body needed and wanted this and only from Dayton.

Before she could come down from the high of her intense release, she felt Dayton move behind her and in one long surge, nine and a half inches of pure, unadulterated manhood entered her from behind. Kima felt her body being moved until she was settled on her knees, ass up in the air and her face down on the mattress. The picture in her head of what they looked like had her body reaching for her next orgasm as if one hadn't just shattered her into a million little pieces.

Dayton tried to hold off and take their night slow. The moment he checked into their suite earlier in the day before Kima arrived, he couldn't wait to sink into her welcoming body. He was now getting his wish.

Looking down at her as his hips flowed back into him, he watched the area where their bodies were joined. He delighted in the wet, silkiness from her body that coated his penis. With each move in and out of her body, the wetness increased. Loving Kima like this was one of their favorite positions. He hadn't planned on getting to this point just yet, moving from tasting her to entering her, but when her body creamed onto his fingers and tongue, the taste of her drove him mad with wanting a more intimate connection. It took him seconds to slide his boxer briefs down, joining them where they now loved like they never wanted to stop.

With precise strokes, he loved her, sliding all the way in before pulling out almost to the point of separating them. That move teased them both. When Kima grimaced at him, he glided back inside of her. Their loving was always in sync. He could feel the sweat forming on his brow though the air in their room was on full-blast.

Dayton crossed his arms so that his right hand gripped her left cheek while his left hand gripped her right. Holding her tight, he gave her all of him as he felt her body's sensual walls gripping him before loosening and then gripping him again with each pass into her body.

His grunts accompanied Kima's moans of pleasure. When she screamed for more, he gave her more. When she yelled for harder, he increased the strength behind the rush of his hips. Seconds later, he felt Kima's body give into her second release as she flopped about on the bed, calling and screaming his name.

"Yes, baby! Yes!" Dayton yelled just before his own body let go and rockets shattered across his eyelids. With uncontrollable, powerful strokes so fierce to the point that he wanted to pull back to not love Kima too hard, Dayton felt his body emptying into Kima's with a force that had his legs shaking and quaking as his orgasm pierced his very soul. There wasn't a part of him that wasn't a part of his release. The sound of their bodies slapping together and Kima continuing to scream his name had him forgetting to pull out. He couldn't stop. Kima's body was the haven where he found everything he'd ever wanted in a woman. Loving her like this never had a limit and he wouldn't start now.

As his body calmed while attempting to control his ragged breathing, Dayton rolled them to the side so that his body spooned Kima's. He pulled her as close to his body as he could while lavishing her skin with kiss after kiss. With their bodies still intimately connected, he waited a few minutes as they both worked to come down from the enjoyable height of loving each other.

Kima was ready. There was no way she could keep what was in her heart inside of her any longer. She held onto the arm that Dayton rested across her body.

"Day?" she asked sweetly, pulling his attention.

"Mmm, yes, baby," he whispered in her ear.

Kima hesitated for a minute. Taking in a huge gulp

of air, knowing that when they met, Dayton had been one of the biggest ladies' men she'd ever known. She was hesitant and fearful of what his response would be to what she was about to say. There was something about being in Paris and in his arms that made this the perfect moment."

"Kima?" he asked when she didn't say anything after calling him by his nickname.

"Dayton, I love you. I know we didn't set out on a road to love. I also know that we've said we love each other often. None of this was planned when we met. I gather that it was more about lust than anything else, considering we had the most amazing sex the night of our first date. I've never been *in* love before. I've never wanted to be *in* love like I am with you. Here I am, though. I love you. I'm *in* love with you. Using the word, '*in*', means something extra. This may be a crazy moment to declare that, but I need you to know that I don't love haphazardly or this intensely. I know I'm in love with you."

Kima held her breath and then she felt his smile against her neck.

"Kima, I'm *in* love with you too, baby. I'm not saying it just because you said it or because I am literally still inside of you. I'm saying it because I am *in* love with you to the point that I hate when we're apart. You and I both know who I am or who I used to be."

"That man with women at every race who kept his body satisfied? That person?" she asked, grinning facetiously.

"Yeah, that guy. I've always had a vivacious sexual appetite. I used to watch my brothers sneak girls onto the ranch for wild sex and a few times, I watched it all unfold. They didn't care. They were who they were. My mother didn't like it, but my dad knew he could keep an eye on my brothers' comings and goings with it came to women. When I realized the attention my name brought me with girls, that was all I needed to know to get what I saw them getting. I'm not that person anymore; I hope you believe that. I don't want anyone but you and that's a first for me."

Dayton pulled her closer and Kima kissed his arm.

"I know who you were. I also know that the guy you were is not who you are with me. We've been sharing something special since the moment I saw you when I first started attending races. I never wanted to go before. It never really interested me. After meeting you, I never missed any of your races."

Dayton thought of something else special they shared. He needed to get this out now.

"Baby, I didn't use a condom and I didn't pull out like I should have. I have no excuse other than I couldn't stop loving you. Your body had me caught up. I promise you that I'm clean and you are the first person that I've ever had sex with without protection. I'm sorry that I didn't do a better job of protecting you."

Kima separated their bodies, turned and faced him.

After kissing him sweetly on the lips, she made sure their eyes were locked on each other.

"Please don't be sorry for loving me to the point that we both slipped up. I, like you, was caught up in the moment. I'm clean too and that is all we need to worry about."

Dayton looked at her questionably.

"Not all, though," he said.

Kima caught on quickly.

"Right. There is that," she said, nipping at her bottom lip.

"If you're pregnant, we will be okay. We're in this together," Dayton professed before doubt seeped into the moment.

"I'm sure we're fine on that front. I love you. If I'm pregnant, I know we weren't planning for it, but I would never be sorry if I was," she said.

Kima waited for his reaction.

"Me either. I've never thought of anything other than racing before meeting you. What we have is more than racing to me ever has been. That is a lot from a kid who has thought of nothing but racing since I was five years old. You'll tell me if you're pregnant?"

"You will be the second or maybe the third to know. That is, if I have to have it confirmed by a doctor. For now, let's enjoy the rest of this week and not worry about that. Besides, you felt amazing inside of me. On my agenda is to make sure I get some kind of birth control. I got so comfortable with the boxes of condoms you always have; I mean cases. That day I saw your collection in your closet, I had no idea men kept that many. Then I realized, this was Dayton Sullivan, the guy who used to leave a trail of smile on beautiful women's faces. Now, that's reserved just for me and I know it. If we're going to do this love thing, I want us to be comfortable loving each other this way."

Dayton rolled Kima under him and plundered her mouth over and over. He settled his body comfortably between her legs, feeling his body rising to the occasion yet again. Reaching into the nightstand, he grabbed a condom this time. Slipping it on quickly, he spread Kima's legs and easily entered her wet and waiting body. As her arms went around his neck, he knew baby or not, Kima was his forever love and he wasn't going to let anyone or anything keep them apart.

6

Two months later - Australia race

"Oscar! Andrew here. I'm glad to catch you in."

Oscar grumbled under his breath. He had been avoiding Andrew's call since his last trip back from South America over a week ago, his third there in the past few months. He knew that the man was getting anxious about what was going on with Kima's constant ignoring of calls from Nelson. She was messing up his plans to marry her off and, in more ways, than one, get her out of his hair. He was having a hard time keeping Kima in check. She'd been doing a lot of disappearing the past few months and he didn't like it. He wondered if she was still unaware that he knew that she had been seeing Dayton for some time while acting like she was into the idea of marrying Nelson. He didn't know how else to remind her of the dire need he had to make the merger of their two families work.

He put a phony smile on his face for this call, even though they couldn't see each other. He needed the image of himself that way in order keep a straight face while talking.

"Andrew, yes, I've gotten all of your messages.

There is a big race coming up tomorrow morning. A lot is riding on this one, as you know."

"Yeah, I heard about that. I can't believe you actually bet against your own team. I don't know how you plan to win considering that Dayton fella is primed to win yet again. If he wins, you lose. What are you doing and should I get in on it?"

Oscar grumbled under his breath.

"Whatever do you mean?" he asked inanely.

What? Did you convince your guy to throw the race? Is he going to purposely lose so that you can get richer? You know your loan with me is coming due. The only way to pay it off, other than actually paying me, is to get your daughter to set a wedding date with Nelson. That way her money becomes a part of my family while making you a very rich man. I want the raceway that she owns. Does she even understand the value in those tracks? I know her mother didn't. I'll never understand why she would leave it to a girl as naïve as Kima."

"I'm still wondering why that old man left it to Kima's mother, Hydea. I guess he never planned on dying where she would actually end up with everything. It looks like he left it to his son with a little to Hydea and then the son died with him. It's crazy, I guess," Oscar suggested.

"I guess that's one way of going from poor to rich overnight. She certainly did," Andrew offered.

Oscar leaned back in the chair in his home office and looked to the two beautiful women who sat in the outer office waiting on him. He'd paid a lot of money for their time. Andrew was getting on his nerves always barking out orders.

"I'm working on her. She has no idea about the value behind anything she has. She's as stupid as her mother was when it comes to business and finances."

"Then get her to call Nelson. I spoke with him just this morning. He said he's been trying but Kima won't call him back. I also heard a rumor about her and that Dayton fella. Did you know they've been banging it out for months? Maybe even as much as a year? Nelson told me."

Oscar pulled the phone away from his ear in disgust.

"Did you just use the words, *banging it out*, in reference to my daughter?" Oscar scolded.

"Oh, now you're claiming her lovingly as your daughter. That's funny! Use whatever words you want, you know what I mean."

Oscar exhaled loudly. He wondered how Nelson found out. He, himself, had suspected some months back and then he caught Dayton at her apartment one night and knew it was true. He was still trying to figure out how Dayton was able to get out of Kima's apartment before he arrived at her door that morning. He hadn't told Kima he was stopping by. The night before he had spotted Dayton looking out from Kima's balcony. Neither of them had suspected that he'd been keeping an eye on them after he saw odd looks between the two of them at a few of the races. He had also supposed something was up when Kima started traveling to races; something she never wanted to do before. Yeah, he knew and he was already working to put a stop to it. He had a feeling that things were getting serious between them. He had to stop it by any means necessary. Still, he didn't need Andrew knowing that he knew.

"I don't know anything about that. I haven't seen them together and I'm her father," Oscar explained.

"Fathers don't know and see everything. That isn't even the rumor I was talking about," Andrew said cleverly.

"What then?" Oscar waved a few fingers at both girls who were in their early twenties with bodies that wouldn't quit. After he indulged in a little bit of paid fun with them, he had a job that he needed them to do to get Kima away from Dayton. His ultimate plan would make sure that the kid was never a thorn in his side or a wrench in his plans for Kima ever again. For now, he had to turn Kima away from him.

"I have my sources that tell me Kima is pregnant. We both know it's not by Nelson. How true do you think that is?" Andrew asked.

Oscar was so shocked at what he was hearing that he stood faster than he had planned and nearly fell over, bracing himself on the edge of the brown wood desk. The chair under him fell backwards and the glass of tequila he'd prepared, and had yet to drink, tumbled over and spilled on the papers on his desk.

"That's a lie!" he shouted. "Kima wouldn't be that stupid. She knows what it means for her to marry Nelson. I shared that putting them together would make us both rich beyond our wildest dreams."

What Oscar failed to share as that Kima didn't care about being rich. She had a monthly stipend that she would continue to receive from her mother's estate that kept her very comfortable with the kind of life she liked to live.

"Right, right," Andrew snickered. "You mean it would make you rich. I know you, old boy. You're going to rob that little girl blind after she marries Nelson. She won't have to worry about it because Nelson, as my son, will be rich. He'll take care of her, if that's what he chooses. He's actually a lot like his old man. I've been married for a lot of years and I don't think that there has ever been a month that I've been faithful to my wife. She doesn't care as long as she can shop until her heart and *my* wallet are satisfied. I'm sure Nelson will find it delightful to be rich and have women falling at his feet. I don't care what he does as long as I get her racing business. I still can't figure why her mother would leave it to her and not to you. You must have been a lousy husband!" Andrew shouted.

"Well, if I was, it doesn't matter now. She's not here anymore to complain," Oscar reveled.

Hydea may have been a beautiful woman, but what Oscar loved most was her naïveté along with how he dominated her in bed. He didn't miss either once he found out she was scheming against him to expose the underbelly side of his business dealings.

"Yeah, I guess you took care of that."

Oscar didn't respond. Anyone could be listening. He would never speak of what happened to Hydea.

"Listen, whatever you heard about Kima isn't true. If she was pregnant, she would tell me; I'm her father."

"Don't be stupid. You're an intelligent and resourceful man. That little filly of yours has been spreading eagle with Dayton for months and months. You should know that I have people watching her. I know for a fact that two months ago, they spent an entire week in Paris. They barely left their suite. No telling how many times they worked on conceiving that little seed I heard is growing inside of her. I'm only going to warn you one time; if she is pregnant, get rid of that baby. She can't be pregnant with that boy's baby when she is set to soon be engaged to my son. How would that look? If she's not pregnant, figure out how to get rid of this Dayton fella. I know he's your big money maker, but he's a liability. I owe some pretty big people in Russia, South America and the United States. I'm buried up to my ears in guns being pointed at my head and those of my family. A gun pointed at me is two pointed at you and your daughter."

Oscar didn't want to play his hand. He also didn't care about Andrew's threats or warnings. He had to keep the farce going that he didn't know what Kima has been up to. Her possibly being pregnant was a new one for him. How did he let that get by him? He also has had eyes on her and Dayton. He knew about her trip to Paris. She told him she was going with those two best friends of hers, Nala and Bridget. He knew it was a lie. Kima had even gone as far as bringing both girls to his house where they talked about their trip to Paris, which was clearly for his listening pleasure.

He had to admit that he'd been too busy checking out Nala's rack to focus on their conversation. At twenty-nine, that woman had a body that he'd love to see divested of every stitch of clothing. He knew he could be able to turn Nala's head his way if he wasn't old, chubby and creepy-like. More than once, he'd heard her refer to him that way when she didn't know he was listening to her conversations with Kima.

"Don't threaten me, Andrew. I'm doing everything I can to get her in line with this wedding," Oscar lamented.

"Good. Do it soon. I want them at the justice of the peace within a month."

"A month? That's too soon!"

"Oscar, old man, old buddy of mine – you get that girl of yours in front of a justice of the peace with my son in a month or that attorney of your wife's won't be the only body at the bottom of the Mediterranean Sea. I guess those bricks and chains have done wonders for keeping his body lost all this time. Make it happen and do it soon. We have big business to take care of. The next drug shipment is coming through soon and the cars need to be packed and ready to go. The weapons are already on their way. We paid a lot for that cargo shipment as well as to those men who are flying the plane. You need to be on board once the money comes in. The money from these transactions has to be cleaned through your company. Do it Oscar! Do it all now!"

Before he could answer, Andrew ended their call. Oscar was fuming. He missed the days of having a landline phone in his office that he could slam down hard when he was frustrated. He hated being told what to do. Hydea used to try that to keep him in line knowing she owned everything. She had him at her beck and call. He wanted and needed to be his own man. The only way to do that will be to marry Kima off, get her company merged with Gaynor's and then get his cut so that he could disappear and live a life of luxury far from all of this. First, he needed to find out if the news that Andrew shared with him about Kima being pregnant was true or not.

"How could she defy me?" he shouted before swiping his hand angrily across his desk, knocking everything to the floor. "Edna!" he shouted for his housekeeper.

Within seconds, she came running into his office on her little four-foot-ten body.

"Sir?" she asked nervously.

"Clean this up!" he yelled while leaving his office.

He approached the two beauties who sat patiently waiting for him with their arms around each other. He loved the sight of that. In an instant, his anger dissipated and so did the conversation he'd just had with Andrew.

"Oscar, are you ready?" one of the girls asked him, sounding like a kitten, purring at him. He growled back and clawed in the air like a lion would with his paws.

Checking out their outfits, he was glad that they had followed his instructions to wear the skimpiest outfits they could muster up. All he saw was skin and very little fabric – just what he ordered.

"I am. You will have your work cut out for you with me because I'm having a stressful day. I have this room that I call my fun room. Let's go there."

Both girls jumped up on his demand. He pointed them in the right direction as they walked ahead of him. He wanted to have a straight line to their rears as they walked. Checking his pocket for his blue pill prescription, he was all set.

"Edna! Finish up and you can stop working for the day. The walls are not sound proof in this house. It's about to get pretty loud around here!" he yelled and laughed to himself catching up with the girls. Oscar tried hard but he could not remember their names. He didn't care. Their names were not important for what he had in mind. Stepping between them, he wrapped his arms around their waists.

"Is it really a fun room?" one asked.

"It will be for us! After that, I have someone I need both of you to work your magic on. I'm going to need pictures of what you do with him."

"Pictures? Oh, we love pictures!" the other one said. "Pictures will be extra," she added.

Oscar opened the door which led to the lower level of his house after entering the passcode on the keypad.

"I knew it would be extra. As long as you come through, there will be plenty of money on top of what I'll be paying you for our time today. Besides, you will probably enjoy him. You know Dayton Sullivan, the racecar driver?"

"Yeah! He's sexy. He's tall, dark and hot. We hear that he's working with some major equipment. It's him? I'd do him for free, but not this time. This first time, we'll need you to run us the money."

Both girls giggled as he closed the door behind them. Making their way down the stairs, Oscar switched on the lights which illuminated a room on the lower level. Quickly, black walls and red lights gave the dark aura of the space. It may have been dark, but it was created for all things fun. Like he said, his fun room. He'd deal with Kima and her drama later. Getting photos of Dayton in a compromising position may be all that he'll need to do.

Over a year ago, he tried to get some pictures of Dayton that wouldn't make him look good in the media. To his chagrin, there wasn't a woman who had been with him who was willing to do or say anything that could hurt Dayton. He needed a way to get Dayton under his thumb in order to get control of him. Oscar thought that with the number of women Dayton had been known to bed, someone would be pissed that they didn't get more from him. Apparently, he was a charmer. It surely didn't take much to get Kima in bed. He was hoping the two beauties who were checking out all of the *essentials* in the room would be able to come through for him. If not, he had a backup plan; one that Dayton won't escape from. He's done it before and he'll do it again if it means he will secure his bag and his future, as the kids would say.

7

Kima walked nervously up the six concrete stairs to the front door of her father's house. She didn't know how he would take her news, but she knew he needed to know.

The night before, as she lay in Dayton's arms after he'd cooked her a dinner of baked lasagna and fresh garlic bread, a recipe he told her he gotten from the woman who has been cooking for his family since before he was born, she told him that he was going to be a father. Their week in Paris two months ago had, in fact, produced what would be a son or daughter for them in about seven months.

When she first suspected, after not getting a period after that trip, she waited, wondering if perhaps her cycle had just been late. When she missed it a second time around, she took a home test which came out positive. Then to confirm things, a week ago, she made an appointment with her doctor, who told her that she was definitely pregnant. Kima had been more excited than she thought she would be. The idea had first scared the life out of her. Once the possibility was in the atmosphere, she had reached down to touch her stomach and an excitement like none she'd ever experienced poured from her heart. She was instantaneously in love with the possibility. What didn't surprise her was how excited Dayton was. He had been checking with her since that week knowing that they'd had unprotected sex, not just the once, but a few more times. She was remembering the tub when they took a bath together. There was also the one time on a midnight boat ride they'd taken. That time was amazing under a starry night.

After kissing her senseless, he'd gotten out of bed and danced around the room while she laughed copiously from her vantage point on the bed. When she woke this morning, he was already awake and staring at her. Her body stirred as he kissed her further awake with those magical lips of his. It wasn't often that they spent the night at his hotel when he was in Australia. Last night was a special one. Dayton wanted to wake up with her and his baby in his arms. There was no way she would deny the man she loved that right; she didn't care if her father found out or not.

Kima hadn't told Dayton, but something was nagging at her that her father possibly already knew about them. The few times they talked, the way he questioned her about her whereabouts led her to believe he already knew the answers before asking. Still, she would lie until he called her on it. So far, he hadn't.

Her arriving at his house this morning, hours ahead of the race later today that Dayton had already left to prepare for, was about to be her father's awakening if he wasn't already woke to what has been going on in her life. Using her key, she entered through the large brown and glass door. She headed straight to her father's office, which was the second room down the long white marbled floor hallway. She could hear him talking, so she knew that's where he was. Before she could knock on the semi-closed door, it opened and Edna greeted her with a big smile.

"My child!" she exclaimed. Kima was pulled into a tight hug, the kind she loved.

"Hey, Momma E," Kima's name for her. "I'm glad you're here today. I haven't seen you in a long time. My dad keeps you so busy running errands," Kima said, excited.

"I know. Come out back and see me before you leave. I want to catch up. I have some lemon slices I made. You know you love my iced tea."

"Dad is allowing you to rest and relax? I'm surprised!" Kima joked and looked at Oscar who gave her a silly grin.

"Only today. Tomorrow I'm going to plant new flowers. I want you to see them," Edna said, clapping her hands with bliss.

"I'll be right out after I talk to my dad for a minute."

After Edna walked off, Kima walked over and gave her father a slight hug, not a lovingly one, but the kind she's been giving him since losing her mother. She didn't trust him, but he was still the only father she knew; at least for now. She hadn't told him that in the papers she found at his house in a box, she found clues to finding out who her biological father was. There was nothing earth-shattering, but every little bit of information would help. She would keep that to herself for now. There was no way she was going to go through life with Oscar being her only family. It was hard enough that the man who fathered her mother had kept her mother a secret for so long that his family wanted nothing to do with them. That left her with just Oscar, since her mother's family was still in Brazil somewhere, not even knowing she existed.

"Well, what brings you here so early in the morning? There's a race today. I take it you're coming to it?" he asked.

"I am."

"What about to Canada next week? That's our next big race."

"Yes, I plan to go to that race too. After that, I'm going to spend some time with Nala in Florida. We want to hang out in Miami on the beach for a week or so; maybe even longer. I love the United States and their beaches."

Kima sat down in the chair in front of his desk and kept herself from making eye contact after she'd just lied. She didn't want to tell him that she was going with Dayton to his family's ranch in Montana for his brother

Nick's wedding. He would be angry enough in just a few minutes.

"I'm sure that will be fun. I like Nala," he said.

Kima felt a direct feeling of dread as her stomach played tricks on her. She would say it was the baby and morning sickness, but it wasn't. She knew that her father had a thing for Nala, which she hated. It was in his gaze and greeting whenever she was around. Her friends didn't call him creepy for nothing. He eyed her friends like he was always picturing them naked. He didn't know that she knew about his little room in the basement of his house. Some things they just never talked about and that was one.

"Yeah, we're looking forward to having a blast."

"Just you and her? No one else?" Oscar asked.

Kima's eyes did lock with his, this time. She saw something strange in them as if he were trying to read her mind.

"No, just us."

"Good. I know you'll have fun. There isn't another race for a few months after that. To what do I owe this visit, not that I'm complaining about seeing you? You seem to have this knack for disappearing in recent months."

Kima trembled nervously, but knew that she had to get it out in a way that resembled ripping off a band-aid. She moved to the edge of her seat while wiping her sweaty palms on the pink pants of her sweat suit. Readying herself, she exhaled deeply.

"I've been seeing someone. You're going to be mad because it's not Nelson. I don't want to marry him, even though I know that was your plan. I know you said I have to do it. I've heard your reasons but I can't marry a man I don't love. I'm in love with someone else," she said, without speaking Dayton's name. She needed the fact that she was seeing someone, and that it wasn't who he wanted, to sink in first.

"Kima, you can't be in love with someone else. Well, you can be, I guess, but I don't care about that. I do care about the fact that, in love with someone else or not, you are going to marry Nelson. You need to settle down, become a wife and mother. It's time. Nelson will make a good husband. He'll provide well for you."

Kima was surprised about her father's even tone. Him being emotionless so far, was a bit scary. She thought he would fly off the handle like he often did with her.

"This is not the stone age. Women don't marry for business reasons to merge families anymore. That's some mafia type stuff. I can choose who I want to love and marry," she exclaimed defiantly.

She watched her father lean back in his chair while staring at her without even blinking. That was a sign that he was fire-mad, but in control of his anger.

"This is about Dayton, right? You think I don't know you've been sleeping with him for months? I knew it was going on, but love? Is that who you are claiming to love? That boy doesn't love women! He screws them and moves on to the next one. I've heard he's a fan of threesomes with two women. Do you have any idea of the reputation he's acquired in the racing circuit? I once heard someone say they saw him having sex with two women on the hood of one of his cars in the garage at Germany before after one of his races a few years ago. Women love being a notch on his bedpost. Dayton doesn't mind fulfilling those wishes. You can't be in love with a womanizer like that."

Kima gripped the arms of the chair so tight that her perfectly manicured nails dug into the dark wood. She hated that he could get a rise out of her like this.

"Stop it, dad! He is not like that anymore. We all have our secrets and lives to live. He had a right to do whatever he wanted to do and with whomever he wanted to do it with. It was all consensual. I know all about that. Dayton and I don't have any secrets."

"Oh? I hear he spent the night with two beautiful women just last night while you and Nala were at the movies. Did you know about that? You think he loves you back? You're a plaything to him. You will marry Nelson and you'll do it within the month. I've spoken and that's all I have to say about it."

Kima knew that under any other circumstances, she would have questioned her father tossing out an outrageous story like that. Too bad it didn't get a rise out of her like he expected. She knew that Dayton had not spent the night with two women. She had been with him all evening and all night. Her father didn't know that when he texted her the day before and she told him she was out shopping and then headed to the movies with Nala that she had been lying.

With each passing day, Kima saw a side of her father she didn't like. When she told him, just now, that she and Dayton had no secrets, she wasn't lying about that part.

Prior to joining him at his hotel, two women mysteriously showed up in the gym at the race track where Dayton loved to workout. He told her that he thought it was odd that no one else was there working out. He headed to grab a shower before meeting her to cook her dinner when two women appeared in the locker room offering themselves to him. Little did her father know that Dayton had mentioned that two women propositioned him and he laughed it off knowing that at one time in his life, he would have been all over them. Like she just said to her father, Dayton wasn't like that anymore, unless it involved her. She loved and trusted him with her life and the life of their child. What she would not do is marry Nelson; ever.

"I'm not marrying Nelson and you can't make me. I am *not* my mother. You led her around on a string like a puppet for years. I'm no longer allowing you to try and do me the same way. I'm in love with Dayton and in seven months, he and I are going to have a baby."

That was it. The words were out. In the next instant, Kima didn't know what to do as her father stood up suddenly and raced around the desk coming right up into her face. He was so close, she could smell the liquor on his breath. Her stomach began doing summersaults. Clearly, the baby didn't like the stench either.

Kima quickly braced his hands on the arms of the chair, holding on tight. She had never seen him move that fast without being out of breath. The way he was blocking her in, she wouldn't be able to stand and get away from him if she tried. For the first time, she saw rage well up in her father and it was directed toward her. She didn't feel safe.

"Pregnant? Over my dead body, you *tramp*! You let that boy knock you up? He knows what you're worth. He knows you have millions. You think he doesn't want you for that?" Oscar asked harshly.

Kima tried to duck from the brazen way he was speaking to her.

"He's not! Dayton is rich in his own right. His family has more money than you and me put together. He doesn't need or want my money when he has his own that he never taps into. He doesn't have to race for a living. He does it because he loves it. You of all people know that his family is the biggest sponsor of his cars in every race. The Sullivan Ranch name is written in big white letters on every single one of his cars. He doesn't need any of my money. He loves me and I love him. I'm going to have his baby and you can't make me do otherwise."

"You b..."

Kima slammed her hands down hard on the arms of the chair.

"Don't you *dare* call me that! I have never disrespected you. I'm going to ask that you not call me out my name. Please move so that I can get up. It's clear you need to calm down and think clearly. I guess it's too much for you to be happy about being a grandfather."

Kima huffed in frustrated. She had hoped for a different response, but she was glad she prepared for any.

"You're not going anywhere until we get on the phone and you make an appointment to get rid of that thing growing in you. Next, you're going to call Nelson and set a date for a wedding. Following that, you're never going to see Dayton ever again. If you try, not only will you regret it, but Dayton will regret it as well. You do not want me to unleash my wrath on him." Oscar spewed out right into her face.

Kima sat motionless for a few moments before trying to move her body so that her face was not directly lined up with his. She hadn't realized until now just how gross he was.

"I thought this news would make you happy, but I guess not. I love Dayton and nothing anyone says is going to change that.

With her eyes matching his glare, Kima watched Oscar stand to his full six-foot height as he moved away from her.

"You have no idea what you're doing. You're putting both of our lives at risk," he spoke softer.

"Why am I at risk because of the things you've done?"

"Kima, trust me, you have to marry Nelson. If you don't, neither of us will live to see that baby. You have to do this; you must!" he shouted.

Kima lurched out of her seat when he shouted at her. She took this chance to move near the door, giving herself a chance to run out if he approached her again.

"You'll have to fix whatever you've gotten yourself into. I'm going to live my life my way. My way is a life with Dayton and our child. It's up to you if you choose to be a part of this or not."

Before he could answer, Kima turned and opened the door. Before exiting, she watched him forcefully sit down in his chair with his head in his hands. Whatever he has done must be as bad as her mother warned her about. She didn't care, she had to get out of the house.

"Get out, Kima! You're killing us both and you don't even know it. Just get *out*!" Oscar bellowed so loud, the door vibrated.

Kima held her head up high. She even held back the tears that threatened to well up in her eyes. His words and behavior were cutting into her deep. Still, she would not be deterred.

"Tell Edna I'll see her another time," she grumbled out.

Closing the door behind her, Kima was sad she

wouldn't be able to share her good news with Edna. She would do that on a day when her father wasn't at home. As she reached the front door, about to break down in tears, she realized that her father was the only family she had. She needed to convince him to be happy that she was happy. She couldn't leave like this. Turning back around, she made her way back down the hall to his office. She stopped right outside of his door when she heard him talking and Dayton's name came up. Putting her ear to the door she listened.

"Yes, I said you have the green light. I need you to make sure Dayton doesn't get out of this race alive. I don't want him just hurt, I need him dead. He's ruining everything! I thought I could convince my daughter to come to my way of thinking, but she's as insolent and rebellious as her mother used to be. The only way to get what I need is if he dies today during the race. You had a chance to rig the car last night when I had the track cleared. Did you do it?" Oscar asked.

Kima couldn't hear the other end of the phone conversation. She was so scared, she put her hand over her mouth to quelch her cries as tears streamed down her face. Her father was going to do something to Dayton; he had someone do something to Dayton's car.

"Okay, good. You'll be in the stands and when his car comes around your side, let's say for the third leg, blow that bastard to hell! He's been screwing my daughter and got her pregnant. Baby or not, she's going to marry Andrew's son. With Dayton out of the

way, she won't have anyone but me to fall back on. He dies today, is that clear?" Oscar shouted.

Not needing to hear any more, Kima raced down the hall, glad she'd worn soft soled sneakers so that her father wouldn't hear that she'd still been in the house. Once outside after letting the door close quietly behind her, she raced down the steps and around to the side of the house where she'd parked her black BMW 8 Series Coupe.

Hopping inside while breathing hard and out of control, with nervous fingers, she dialed Dayton's phone. She cursed herself when she remembered that he always turned his phone off right before a race so that he could focus. She was too far away to get to the track before he got in his car to practice. She didn't know if whatever someone placed in his car would blow up on its own or not. She had to stop Dayton from getting in the car; she had to. She knew who to call. Searching her contact list, she found the number she needed. Seconds later, a friendly voice was on the other end.

"Rusty?" she yelled louder than she had planned.

"Kima? Are you alright? You never call me," Rusty said.

She couldn't speak when an image of Dayton dead lying on the track flooded her head. She did breakdown, sobbing while feeling the need to break free.

"*Help* me!" was all she could get out before lifting

her hand to cover her mouth. That's just how frightened she was.

"Kima? What's wrong? Has something happened to Dayton? Little One, I need you to calm down. I can hear you crying. What's going on?" Rusty asked.

"It's Dayton!" she screamed.

"Dayton? What happened to him?"

"I don't know. I mean, I think nothing yet. I told my father I was seeing him and that I was in love with him. He was so mean to me. He threatened me and the baby, and Dayton too. He told me to get out of his house. Then I heard him tell someone on the phone that he had a green light to kill Dayton by rigging his car somehow. I think with a bomb or something. I don't know. Please do something Rusty! I can't reach Dayton," she balled even louder.

"I know. He turns his phone off. I don't think your father is that crazy over you being pregnant."

"It's not just that. It's about me marrying Andrew Gaynor's son, Nelson. Something about if I don't marry him, I'm killing us both. My father is into some really bad stuff. He thinks getting Dayton out of the way will make me turn to Nelson. That's what he needs and wants. I'm telling you, he sent someone to do something to Dayton's car last night."

Kima waited through the silence of Rusty not saying anything.

"Dayton is his big money maker. He wouldn't dare," Rusty tried to explain.

Still, Kima heard a questioning tone to his voice.

"He needs Dayton to go away, Rusty. It's bigger than the race."

"Wait. Last night, your father had everyone clear the track for some kind of maintenance before today. That would have left Dayton's care vulnerable. Look, I'm heading to the track right now. Dayton was going to the gym first like he always does. He won't get to the track for another half-hour. I'm going to drive like a bat out of hell, but I'll reach him. Don't you worry."

"Thank you for believing me."

"You love him. That's all I need to know."

Kima smiled into her phone. Rusty believed her.

"Thank you," she smiled and said.

"The way that boy loves you, I know you wouldn't call me unless it was dire important. This definitely is. You can't stay here, Kima. You have to go. I need you to get everything you can and meet me and Dayton at the airport. I'm getting both of you out of Australia today; right now!"

"What about Canada? That's his next race," she said.

"Dayton isn't going to care about that. When I talk to him, all he will want to know is that you are safe and away from Oscar. He would kill me if I didn't keep you out of harm's way. Where are you right now?" he asked.

"Sitting on the side of my father's house in my car. I ran outside and called you. I haven't driven off yet."

"Good. Don't go home yet. I'm going to send Travis

and Kendall, two members of my security team to help you get yourself and your things to the airport. I'll have someone else go pack up Dayton's hotel room. Don't talk to anyone; I mean no one, Kima. Don't tell anyone what you just told me. I have been telling Dayton for months that Oscar has been rubbing me the wrong way lately. I even heard he bet against Dayton in today's race. That should have been a flag for me. Now you tell me this? If this is true, I don't know who else Oscar has in play."

Hearing the fear in Rusty's voice elevated her own fear. Kima bounced around in her seat. She needed to have her eyes set on Dayton. She needed him so much; she loved him so much.

"Where will I go?" she asked, scared out of her wits.

"Your friend who sometimes comes to the races here with you. Who is that?"

"That's Nala. She's my best friend."

"Call her and go to her house. Text me the address. Leave your car there and Travis and Kendall will know what to do. I don't know all of what's going on here, but to be safe, you and Dayton need to disappear right now."

Kima could hear the wheels of Rusty's car as he raced through traffic. She herself exited her father's block and headed for Nala's flat. She didn't have to call her since she had her own key to get in.

"Where will we go, Rusty?" she asked as she placed one hand over the baby, feeling the need to be extra protective.

"The only safe place I know that you will both be safe; the Sullivan Ranch in Montana. Nobody messes with them; nobody at all," Rusty declared.

Kima nodded and drove safely. Ready or not, she was about to meet the Sullivan family. She was sad that she was bringing drama to their doorstep, but happy that, if nothing else, Dayton would be safe from her father's wrath. She couldn't lose the man she loved; that was not an option.

As she drove, she was reminded that she'd already lost her mother, most likely at the hands of her father. She would not let Dayton fall the same way. She would do exactly as Rusty said. She would wait and meet him and Dayton at the airport, putting Oscar and all this mess behind her. Her life didn't have to be in Australia. It was wherever Dayton was. According to Rusty, that place was with his family. She was ready.

8
Present Day
Sullivan Ranch, Bozeman Montana

Marta Sullivan moved so fast around her industrial sized kitchen that her husband, David Sullivan stood back with his hands up in a surrender stance. She knew she looked like a mad-woman banging and clanging pots and pans as if she were losing her mind. When it came to her kids, she would go mad-crazy on any and everyone. The idea that a man who threatened the life of her son was on her loving ranch had her steaming. Her husband's excuse didn't sit well with her. The last thing she wanted was someone on her ranch who would do harm to anyone, especially her family.

"Marta, can you stop moving for a minute and talk to me? It's the middle of the night and you have to be tired after Nick and Parker's wedding and reception earlier today," David suggested.

Turning briskly, Marta knew her gaze fused through David and pierced his heart. She could tell by the look in his eyes. Usually, they were able to talk about anything, but this was about a man who tried to kill her son now on the ranch where her son was sleeping in his own house. Dayton had arrived with a woman he was obviously in love with and who was also pregnant with his child, she had been told; another grandchild for her. When she should be happily living on cloud nine with two sons married, two grandchildren, by way of Gizelle, and then with her being pregnant with Perry's first child, bad news had to be thrown in. Despite that, she was also elated that another grandbaby was on the way. Her happiness was interrupted with the thought that Dayton could have died and he would have been thousands of miles away.

"Talk? What is there to talk about? Why would you bring that man onto the ranch? You could have dropped him in a hotel. Why here?" she pleaded.

"Not so loud. Don't forget Carrie and Brody are asleep upstairs. We had already agreed to babysit for Gizelle and Perry before all of this happened. You don't want to wake them up."

"Well, you should have thought of that before you brought this man onto this ranch. How could you? Not only are my kids here, but my grandchildren are asleep right upstairs, as you just reminded me. You have the nerve to bring some lunatic here. You know this kind of person isn't allowed."

David wished there was something he could say or do to calm his wife. He has learned over the years to just let her get it out.

"Honey, come sit down in the family room. Let me explain everything that happened and then what

Dayton told me. I don't plan on this man, Oscar, being on the ranch for long," he explained guiding her into the other room. Once seated, he started off explaining everything to her, but then she said more and he waited his turn to speak.

"This better be good to keep me from walking out of here and to the cabin where you put him up. I want to throttle him! He tried to hurt my baby boy!"

David chuckled. He loved the fire in his wife. No one messed with her cubs. Oscar had no idea that Marta is the person he needs to fear the most and not him and his sons.

"I know, I know. Calm down. Listen, I told you, I brought him on the ranch to be looked at. I knocked him out, sweetie. I was just as mad as you are right now. I couldn't hold back that right hook even if I tried. I saw a flash of my son in danger and I just let go. I couldn't drop this man off at some hotel in that condition. He was out cold at the entrance to the ranch. I hit and knocked him out. Did you hear that part?"

Marta huffed.

"You should have. Well, is he okay?" she added.

David relaxed. He knew she was mad. He also knew that he had fallen in love with and married a woman with a kind heart for everyone; even fools like Oscar who brought a knife, words, to a gunfight, David's fist.

"Yes. He's going to be fine. The ranch doctor checked him out. Other than a serious headache, a seriously sore jaw and perhaps a swollen eye, he'll be fine."

"What about Dayton and Kima? Are they okay? Is the baby okay?" she asked.

"Yes, they are all fine. The doc checked her over before tending to her father. She was so wired-up hearing he was here in Montana that Dayton was scared for her and the baby. Brielle was with them. You know how she is about Dayton. Besides being happy that he's home on the ranch, she wasn't letting him out of her sight until she knew he was good. She sent me a text that Kima was asleep and Dayton had just locked up and was heading up to be with her. Kima was really worked up."

"I can imagine. Now, tell me what's going on?" Marta asked.

David took her hand in his and spun her wedding rings around in his fingers as he talked.

"It seems Kima has a letch for a father who is caught up into some very seedy business with a group of unsavory people. He has or had, according to Dayton, a plan to marry Kima off to some man's son even though she's in love with Dayton and carrying his child. Dayton told me that the last day he was in Australia and preparing for a race, Rusty raced up to him and told him that his car for the race that day was possibly tampered with in a manner that he wouldn't make it out of the race alive. This Oscar guy needed Kima to marry this kid named Nelson and of course, she wasn't going to do that. Her father saw Dayton as a threat to his livelihood and schemed to do him harm. Luckily, Rusty got to Dayton in time. The car was checked out and it had been tampered with. Not only that, but there was a device found on the car that, using some kind of remote, would have blasted the engine, making the car catch on fire and potentially explode and kill our son. Rusty didn't know what else was coming in the wings, so he put Dayton and Kima on a private plane and sent them here. Dayton was planning on coming here anyway for the wedding. They actually arrived a few days ago and stayed at a hotel just to get their heads in order before coming here to the ranch. According to Perry, who asked him about that, Dayton explained that he just needed a minute. So much had happened. He knew he could get rest here on the ranch, but he just needed some quiet time with Kima."

"What? What do you mean he went to a hotel instead of coming here? That boy is definitely our wild child. His one and only stop should have been right here. Wait until I get my hands on him in the morning," Marta fumed.

"There is no need for violence against your son. You know the minute you see him, you'll cry and hug him so tight that he'll struggle to breathe. He's here; he's home and he's safe. Most of all, he's in love and will be a father. We should be celebrating, not trying to strangle him for not coming right home. He knew that once he reached the ranch, there would be people everywhere. More than that, there would be questions he wasn't ready to answer. He just wanted to have some quiet time with his woman after what they had been through. He's still young and learning his way. Give him that, please, honey," David pleaded.

"Well, he can always have that here. He didn't need to stop in a hotel first. If this is about what I think it's about when you say some alone time, I know you let those boys run free when it came to girls and sex on this ranch."

David chuckled and Marta playfully slapped his arm and laughed with him.

"It's the Sullivan way. I had boys and hormones everywhere. I needed to keep a close on their activities. I couldn't do that if they weren't on the ranch," he explained.

"Whatever. Let me just say, Brielle, and I know that will quiet your need to laugh," she said, rolling her eyes and crossing her arms across her chest as she leaned all the way back on the sofa.

"Don't talk about my baby girl and sex in the same sentence. I have a lot of land to bury a body!" David joked. That got a smile out of his wife and that's all he needed.

"Whatever," she replied.

"Give Dayton some room. He will come and talk to you. Be happy he is home. Whatever Kima's father is into, we can keep them safe. There is more Dayton wanted to talk about, but I told him we'll do it tomorrow or in a few days. In the morning before everyone gets up and are moving about, Oscar will be off of our ranch with a warning to not return. He thought that he could come here and make Kima return to Australia with him. You should have seen him demanding that we release her as if we were holding her hostage. We *all* had to keep Dayton from going at the man when it was me that they should have been watching. I saw that grimace on his face when I heard about what he tried to do. Something came over me. I just let him have it. You know I'm not a fighter. Like my boys, us Sullivan men are *lovers!*" David bragged.

"I can't dispute that. I hope those women locked in with our boys for life realize that the love from a Sullivan man does *not* dwindle over the years. You, my love, stay bringing the fire!" Marta quipped before rolling into David's outstretched arms.

"Do you realize that this if the first time in a long time that everyone is on the ranch? Even Shelton is in his house here and not at his favorite place, his downtown top floor condo."

Marta sat straight up.

"Shelton stayed over? Wow, we do have everyone here. Who is watching our guest?"

"He was moved to one of the bunkhouses where the boys will keep a close eye on him until the morning. He'll be escorted off the property to go wherever he wants as long as it's not this ranch."

"You're sure he can't sneak out and try to find Kima

and Dayton?"

"At this hour? He's not going anywhere. Buck has that situation fully under control. If he snores loud, there is someone close by and listening for any movement. You know if I'm here and not there, then I'm good with the security Buck has in place."

"Was this man alone?"

"From what I can tell, yes; that is, so far. I don't know who or what else is coming, but we're ready for it."

"What about Kima? Does she want to leave?"

"Dayton told me that Kima was fine if she never saw him again. This man is actually her stepfather, not her biological father. She doesn't feel safe around him. Not only did he threaten Dayton, but he threatened her life and the life of their baby. You already know Dayton isn't going to let her out of his sight. He's in love. You should see how protective he is over her. I never expected that out of him at this age. I figured he would spend at least the next ten years playing the field. He couldn't wait to get out there and have the kind of uncommitted kind of fun that his brothers all experienced. I know that racing is his life, but falling in love with a woman and having a baby? That surprised me."

Marta stood, satisfied that she'd heard enough.

"Me, too. It is what it is. If he loves her, we love her already too. That's how we Sullivans do. Now, I'm going to go upstairs to check on my grandchildren and to get into bed. Don't you just love the sound of that? One moment, I'm complaining that none of my children have given me grandkids and I already have two with two more on the way. I'm sure by the time Nick and Parker get back from their honeymoon there will be a third one stewing in her belly. Have they not seen how many children you and I had? I hope they're ready for how easily Sullivan men make babies."

"They don't have a clue, honey. You go check on them while I lock up and put away all those pots you took out. Sarah will have a fit when she sees what you did to the kitchen."

Marta moved toward the steps that led up to the bedrooms and she stopped and turned around.

"I am happy that Dayton is home. I don't like the circumstances that brought him here, but still, I'm ecstatic. He has always been the one I worried about the most; even more than Nick when he was fighting fires all the way in New York City. I didn't even worry like this when Perry was up against Gizelle's ex-husband when he wanted to harm her. Like Nick, Dayton couldn't wait to get off of the ranch. I'm just happy that they all know that this is home, no matter what. Do you think that Dayton will consider staying for good? The raceway is being built and he's finally getting his own racing circuit, his own team. That was all his idea and now he can stay here to run it himself. There's also the go-cart track that he talked about since he was a little boy racing box cars. There is so much for him here. Also, whatever Kima wants to do, we are here to help her, especially with the baby."

"Now, he may not want to stay. We talked about this many times before. We want our children to make their own way and find their own dreams, on or off of the ranch. Whatever Dayton decides to do, we will support him."

"He's my baby boy. I've never liked him racing those fast cars. I worried every time I knew a race was coming up. I was nervous at the races I went to watching him drive so fast. I didn't like it but I will always support him. I hope that he at least stays long enough to think about all that he can achieve right here at home with us, Kima and the baby."

"I'm with you, you know that. I want them all close too. It has to be their decision," David said before turning toward the front door to check to be sure it was locked.

"Even Brielle?" Marta said, stopping him from moving.

David knew what she was trying to do, once again, by bringing up their only daughter's name. He'd been guilty of treating his baby girl a little different than his sons. He couldn't help it. She was his only daughter and he would move heaven and earth to keep her safe and yes, close by.

"That's different," he said, not turning around to face his wife's questionable eyes. He already knew what he would find.

"How? How is that different? Because she's a girl? You have spoiled her, in a good way. What happens if she decides to make her life off of the ranch? What will you do?" Marta questioned.

David turned toward her.

"Do you remember what I said after you had Dayton? I told you that I wanted as many babies as it would take to get me a baby girl. I love my boys but there is something about my baby that I fear I would actually kill someone to protect her. The world is a wild and crazy place. It's even harder on women. It's not that I don't think that she could take care of herself. Of course, I know that she can. It's just that she's my baby."

"I know what you're saying. I just want you to know that I feel that way about all of them, from the oldest to the youngest. You have built this ranch and all of its other companies. You did so in hopes that our children would find something in any of them that would sustain them and a future. I want to know that they appreciate what you all have built here and not run away from it. Brielle may want to leave this ranch. What will you do if that's the choice she makes?" Marta asked him.

He didn't have to think about his answer to hard, but David faked like he had to contemplate how he would respond. He then let her have it.

"Well, then, you and I would have to move with her. That's all I'm going to say about it," he jested.

"Silly man!" Marta tossed out at him as she turned and made her way up the stairs. "You are so silly. I love you."

"I love you, too."

9

David was about to check the door when he heard footsteps on the front porch. Peering out, he saw Dayton on the other side of the door. He rushed to open it thinking something was wrong, perhaps with Kima.

"Day? What's wrong? Is Kima okay? The baby?" he questioned, hurriedly.

"Oh, Pop, she's fine. They are both fine. She's sleeping soundly. It's me who can't seem to close my eyes knowing Oscar is on this ranch."

"You know he can't get to you or her, right? There are guys inside the bunkhouse, outside it, two in trucks outside of your house and one in the back in a truck. They won't sleep until Buck tells them they can," David explained, assuring him.

"I know. That's the only reason I left Kima alone at the house. I know the guys would die before letting anything happen to her. I was out walking to clear my head. I still do that no matter where I am. It's a thing. I saw the lights on here at the house and figured, if not mom, then you were still up."

"Come on in, or do you want me to come out?"

David asked.

"Can you come out and walk with me?"

There it was. No matter how grown his sons were, when they needed him and he could hear it in their voices, he didn't hesitate to drop everything for them. This was one of those moments. With Brielle, that was always a given too.

"Sure. Your mother went up to check on the babies. I'm sure she will be sound asleep in a few minutes. She'll want to be up early to be sure Oscar is off of this ranch at first light, which is only a few hours away. Let me set the alarm and I'll join you."

What David didn't say was that he would also grab his gun, just in case. It wasn't often that he wore it on his hip, but having an unwanted stranger on his ranch, he felt it was needed; again, just in case.

Locking up the house and setting the alarm after putting his nine-millimeter in his holster on his right hip, he joined Dayton outside. He thought they were going to walk, but when Dayton sat down on the top step, David didn't question it; he simply sat next to him.

"Pop, how did you know that mom was the one for you? I mean, I know the story of how you met and fell in love, but how did you know?"

"Are you doubting your love for Kima?"

"Not even for a second. I've never felt for any girl or woman the way I feel for her. I've been with a lot of women, you know that, but I've never even once been in love with one of them. I didn't expect to fall in love with her, but it's more than just the physical. I love everything about her. We have fun together and laugh and joke. I listen to her talk about how she never wanted to own a racing circuit. It was left to her by her mother who got it from her own father upon his death some years ago, even though they didn't have a relationship."

"What does she want to do?" David asked.

"She wants to go back to college and get her degree with her focus on getting into law school, passing the bar and being a practicing attorney. She went for two years, then stopped. She said that being a lawyer had been her dream for a long time, but she got caught up in being a rich, party girl; that was until her mother died."

David nodded. He could understand how something like that could steer a person in a different direction.

"I'm sorry she had to go through that.," he said.

"Thanks, Pop. When I met her, she spent most of her time hanging with friends and partying. The first night we went out on a date, we went dancing and I mean, I had not had that good of a time in, well never. I know how to have a good time, but with her, something was different. We talked for hours and hours and hours. When I talk about the track that's being built here on the ranch and how it's my dream to own and run my own team, she pulls more out of me by really listening and giving me feedback. When we're alone, it's like I enjoy shutting out the world and just being with her. She's just a kindhearted person. She reminds me of the kind of woman mom is. I fell in love so fast that at first, my feelings for her scared me. I was ready to run back into the arms of random women, but then I couldn't forget how it felt to just be with her; that was all I wanted."

"She's the one for you, it sounds like. Your story is similar to how I felt about your mother, almost instantly. From the very first moment, there was never anyone else. I wasn't looking and didn't even think about entertaining the idea of anyone else. It was her and only her. My life has been stupid happy since that day. I knew it because my heart knew her heart. The idea of not loving her was hard to bear. I decided I would never let that happen. I will always love her and only her."

"It's like that with Kima, Pop. I mean, when Rusty told me about what Oscar had done to my car once he had it checked out, I was mad, yes, but my first thought was where was Kima and if she was okay. Rusty assured me she was fine. The moment I called her and heard her voice, I felt like I could breathe freely. She was safe. I just wanted to get to her. I didn't care about that damn car or any race or anything. I only cared about getting to her and setting my eyes on her and my baby. Can you believe I'm going to be a father? Crazy, right?" Dayton asked.

David never doubted that any of his sons would make great fathers. They were raised to find the perfect love and treat her like a queen. From there, they would have, and raise amazing kids. He loved his sons not just with the hardness that men think they need to instill in their sons, but with a softness that would allow them to love and appreciate a good woman when they found the one. Like Nick and Perry, Dayton had done just that. Shelton was another story. He hid his personal life with women by spending most of his time in his penthouse condo in downtown Bozeman. Still, David had heard the stories of his son's bachelor life in his bachelor pad.

"Crazy? Yeah, a little because it's unexpected. Like you, we knew racing was your life. I thought you would have a lot more years just focusing on traveling around the world. What I do know is that you will be a wonderful father. I see how happy the idea of it makes you. Even in this darkened night, I can see the gleam in your eyes the moment you mentioned being a father. What you need to think about is, now that you're in love with Kima, what kind of life do you want? What's next for the two of you? Most of all, what the hell has her father gotten himself into and will it continue to disrupt your lives? Is she or you safe if you leave the ranch and head back to where she lives? What are you thinking right now?" David asked.

He knew that the perfect answer from his son would be that he was giving up racing, for now, and staying on the ranch where he belongs. He could figure out the idea of racing once his own raceway was completely. That would certainly appease his mother, but David knew not to nudge him in one direction or another.

He waited as Dayton's head dropped down between his legs which were raised high with his feet propped up on the second step. He let the silence live between them until Dayton was ready to confide in him.

"I love Kima and our baby. I want to marry her and help her live out her dream of going back to school. I want to raise our baby and have more babies together after we're married. I need to keep her and the baby safe from Oscar. I have to get to the bottom of what he's done that would make him want me dead and Kima married to a man she doesn't love. Most of all, for now and until Kima has the baby, we're going to stay here on the ranch. I know they'll be safe. I can't let anything happen to them. I can't let Oscar get his clutches into her."

Dayton paused but David knew something else was weighing on him.

"What is it, Day? I see it in your eyes. Talk to me."

Dayton turned his whole body around and David turned to face him.

"Kima's mother. She died a few years ago and though it was labeled driver error, Kima believes Oscar had her mother killed to protect the secrets of whatever he's gotten himself involved in. She thinks he also had her mother's lawyer killed to keep his secrets from being exposed that her mother may have shared with him in confidence. I wouldn't put it past him to get rid of Kima so that he could get his hands on her money. She's got millions, Pop, and she currently is the owner of record of the Australian raceway and team. Oscar didn't know that her mother changed her will before her death, leaving everything to Kima. He has been running it, but he can't do anything with the business without Kima, unless she is gone too. I haven't said this to her, but I think he would be fine if he could get rid of her. That's why I can't let her go back to Australia just yet. She's safer here. All of us have always felt our safest here at home. I don't know why I had this drive to stay away. Loving Kima and having my baby on the way, I know there is no place I'd rather be than here. I don't know what the distant future holds, but if Kima is open to it, we're staying right here on the ranch. She wants to find her father, her biological father, and I want to help her. She feels like she doesn't have any family."

David put his arm around Dayton's shoulders.

"Son, she has us. You know how this family is. All we need to know is she's the woman you love and she needs us. We're not just your family, we're hers too. Why don't you go get some rest? It'll be daylight soon. Everyone will be refreshed and ready to dive into what we can do to help."

Dayton stood and walked down the steps. Before he got too far, David smiled when he stood and pulled

Dayton into a hug; one that he knew his son needed.

"Thanks, Pop. Thanks for always being you; always being what we all need, when we need it and the way we need it. I needed this hug more than you can imagine. I've missed it. I've missed everyone. I've missed the ranch."

"You're home, son. This is always home for you, Kima and the baby."

Dayton nodded and walked away toward his house on the ranch. It was a house that his mother always kept clean and ready for him for whenever he ventured this way.

Turning to get rest for himself, David first sent a text to Buck to check that things were going alright. When he got the thumbs up right after he sent his text, David smiled and went inside. In a few hours, he would confront a demon on his ranch and decide what his next steps would be.

10

Waking to find Dayton's arms around her holding her close is how Kima was imagining the rest of her life being. Neither of them spoke of the future with all that was going on in the present. Her need to give her body a full body stretch woke the sleeping love of her life.

"You should still be asleep," Dayton uttered close to her ear, nuzzling it.

"I can't sleep with you poking me on the butt. You're naked?" she asked, turning her head to lift the comforter to get a look. She was once again thankful that the morning sun shone bright through the two large bedroom windows of the three-bedroom house that was Dayton's residence on the Sullivan ranch. Even though she hadn't left the house since her father arrived on it a few days ago, she was using the stories that Dayton had been telling her to get a real picture of what it looked like.

"Did you think I was lying when I said I slept naked all the time?"

"Even home on the ranch?" she asked.

"Everywhere. I don't like restrictions when I'm in bed. You know I have no qualms about being bare at any given time."

Kima didn't admit it right away, but she loved him best in all of his naked glory. Dayton's body was meant to be looked at, though she liked to know that the view was being reserved just for her. He had muscles that bulged with delight. Most of his chest and arms were covered in tattoos which she loved running her hands and tongue all over. He once told her the story behind each one. His wasn't just for show – they told of his journey in life so far and his dreams to come. His body, which was in tip-top shape turned heads everywhere he went. She smiled knowing he was all hers.

"Day, I think I want to go out today. I've been in this house for three days, cooped up as if there isn't a world outside. I still haven't had the chance to meet all of your family. They must think I'm a prude staying locked up in here."

Turning fully around, Kima laid her head on Dayton's chest and wrapped her arms around his waist. She was ready to get as naked as he was. Though she was in a short pink satin nighty, she felt overdressed compared to him. Before she could say another word, her morning reminder that she had their baby growing inside of her stirred. She knew that if she didn't make it to the bathroom immediately, she was going to get sick all over Dayton's neatly accommodating bedroom with the dark brown wood furniture and black and gray sheets and comforter.

Tossing back the comforter, Kima covered her mouth just long enough until she reached the bathroom. As the contents of her stomach poured out into the toilet, she was pleasantly surprised, again, to feel Dayton behind her holding back her hair as he slowly caressed her back. Her body convulsed again and again and he never wavered. He held firm, being there for her. Sitting down on the floor instead of on her knees, she waited until the waves of nausea subsided.

"It's okay, baby. I'm right here with you. I hate that this happens to you every single morning. How long is this morning sickness thing supposed to last?" he asked.

Kima didn't know. She hadn't been back to her doctor or any doctor since the day she found out she was pregnant. She was scheduled to have an appointment later this week back in Australia. She knew that wasn't happening. She hadn't even had a chance to fill her prenatal vitamin prescription. Things had moved so fast with them getting out of Australia. She needed to get back on track.

"I don't know. I need to see a doctor. I didn't fill my vitamin prescription. The doctor here on the ranch checked me out the night of the wedding and said I was fine. That wasn't a full exam, though. I haven't had a chance to ask many questions of a doctor since finding out I was pregnant."

"Do you want to see her again? I know she wouldn't mind. She's works here on the ranch and has for a few years. You can't imagine the number of accidents the bunkhouse boys have in a week's time alone," he laughed.

Kima raised her head, sure that the moment had now passed. When she looked up at Dayton, he knew it was time to help her up. For the past few days, this had become a morning ritual for them.

"Do you think she'll see me?" she asked, now on her feet.

Before she could ask him, Dayton had already grabbed two washcloths. One, he ran cold water over and placed it against her forehead after seeing the sweat forming from the exertion she used to toss up last night's dinner of baked chicken, green beans and potatoes that his mother had cooked and sent over to them.

"Of course, she will. I'll give her a call to see if she can come by here."

"Dayton, I want to get out of here. Maybe I can go to her. It's been three days since Oscar was here. He's gone from the ranch now. I'm feeling good enough to go out. Besides, I want to interact with your family. I'm on their ranch and they haven't seen me other than the night of the wedding. Only Brielle and Perry have."

After running the hot water, Kima used the other cloth to wipe it across her face. She smiled when

Dayton was already handing her the toothpaste and a toothbrush, another morning ritual after she came out on the other side of morning sickness. He knew the first thing she would want to do is brush her teeth.

"Baby, you can go anywhere you want to on the ranch. My family not seeing you is my fault. I asked them to give you a little space for a few days. Besides the mess with Oscar, I know the baby is doing a number on you."

"Well, I read somewhere that this should pass after this first trimester. Are you going to finally tell me what happened with Oscar that first morning? We haven't talked about it. I remember you getting up after barely sleeping an hour. Where did you go when you left out?"

"You were awake? I thought you were sound asleep," Dayton uttered.

"I was, but I felt you slip out of bed. Then I heard you close and lock the front door. I did go back to sleep. It seems all this baby wants me to do is eat, toss it up and then sleep all day."

"Today, go out and explore. My sister and my sisters-in-law are all dying to talk to you."

Kima took a moment to try and remember all of their names. She knew Brielle.

"Besides Brielle, that would be Parker and Gizelle, right? I thought Parker was with your brother on their honeymoon."

"They're leaving tonight. Nick wanted to hang around a few days until things calmed and we got some answers."

"Did you get any from my father?" she questioned.

Kima didn't think so, but it was worth a try to ask.

"He claimed he had nothing to do with what happened to my car. I didn't tell him that you overheard him. He doesn't need to know that. I want you as far from what's going on as possible. He did try to threaten us if we didn't turn you over to him. He even threatened to press charges against my father for knocking him out. Too bad for him, there isn't a witness in sight who would offer up any support for what happened to him. I will say that he is a desperate man."

"Start from the beginning," Kima said.

Freshly brushed and feeling minty fresh, she turned around and leaned back against the long white and gray marble bathroom counter top. She loved how spacious it was with its two large sinks with black hardware. The space was all man as she looked around at the same hardware in the shower and around the tub. It splayed out against the wall under a large window that looked out at some of the largest mountains she'd ever seen. She'd almost fallen asleep in that tub the night before until Dayton came in, picked her up, put a nighty on her and placed her in bed. She so wanted him to make love to her, feeling her desire for him rise each time his hands touched her. Before she could utter the words to let him know what she wanted, she'd fallen asleep. That was the last thing she remembered before waking up this morning.

"Okay. You're right that I slept about an hour that night, or early that morning, after I went out and talked to my father. I was only going to go for a walk to clear my head but I saw the lights on in their house and knew one of them must be woke. It was him. I came back here, laid down with you for a bit and watched you sleep. When daylight hit the house, I got up and raced to the bunkhouse. My father and brothers were already there giving Oscar the third degree. He said something about being in debt to some powerful and dangerous men. He came to collect you after he found out where we went. No one told him. He remembered where I hailed from and figured this was where we went when we didn't show up in Canada after missing that last race."

"I wondered what he would think when you missed it, knowing you were pegged to win again."

"Yeah, he started talking about me owing him some money because I was under contract to race and I bailed. He blabbered something about losing a lot of money on both races. He's pissed because the number one draw to the racing circuit right now, me, wasn't there. A lot of the fans walked out after finding out I wasn't racing. When I said he was responsible because of what he tried to do to me, he denied, denied, denied. He said it wasn't him, but that he might know who it was. There is no doubt that it was him. You heard him. We're keeping that bit of information to ourselves. Anyway, there was a lot of back and forth and the bottom line was, Oscar was taken off the ranch and back to his car. It had been towed by Buck to behind the ranch gates until that morning when he was driven to it, told to get into it and go back home. He said he couldn't leave without you or you are both dead. That got a rise out of me. I wanted to lay him out myself after hearing a threat like that from him. He said it wasn't from him but from those he owed. My father warned him about coming anywhere near you or me or he would have the fierce wrath of all of the Sullivan men and then some, on his back."

"My dad is really extra, isn't he? I had no idea this is what my life would turn into. He's an evil man. The way he talked to me in his office that last morning. I was scared to death. He wanted me to terminate my pregnancy. He wanted me to wait around to make an appointment that day. He then said I had to call Nelson to get married in a month at a justice of the peace or some crap like that. He's dangerous Dayton. Stay away from him," Kima declared.

She felt her heart rate speed up at the thought of what could have happened to him if she hadn't doubled back to speak to her father that day. She couldn't bare anything happening to him.

When Dayton moved to where he stood between her partially spread legs and kissed her so lovingly, she didn't want to be anyplace other than with him. His lips parted hers and their love bloomed immediately. The feel of his tongue coaxing hers into a sensual dance is what she needed to take her mind off of any more troubles.

Kima pulled Dayton's body closer to hers and felt his excitement swell.

"Love me," she whispered against his lips, coming up for air. Their kissing was as intense as their lovemaking. No one had ever loved her as intentionally as he does.

"Kima, you were just on your knees tossing out your stomach."

Reaching around she caressed the hard muscles of his behind, pulling his body even closer to hers. He towered over her by over a foot. That part of her that ached to feel him wasn't positioned in the right place to really feel him.

"Up, baby," she slurred sexily against his chest.

Dayton knew what that meant. He would never deny Kima anything she wanted.

Lifting her with little effort, Dayton placed Kima up onto the marble counter in the large space between the faucets. Placing her right at the edge, his body was already positioned to enter her. As wild and sexy as they loved loving each other, he didn't know if rough and wild was the call of the day. He didn't want to harm the baby in any way. When Kima reached to release him and gripped his manhood with both of her hands, stroking him from base to tip, there was no way his body could pull back from rising to please them both. Kima had a way of stroking him that had him at her mercy.

As her hands rotated up and down and around his hardness, he knew he had already lost the unspoken battle.

"Are you sure we shouldn't wait until after the doctor checks you over? The baby," he slurred against her cheek all while his hips moved slightly in and out of her grip. The friction was exactly what he needed to send him over the edge. His woman gave new meaning to what a hand job was. Other women, he'd had to show how to pleasure him this way. Kima went on instinct, paying attention to what had him responding to her the way she wanted in order to know what he loved. Her hands on him like this was at the top of the list.

"Pregnant women have sex every day. They have slow, passionate love and wild, crazy, off the charts sex like we love to have. I want it all. Most of all, I want it right now. It's been days. You can't tell me you're not going stir crazy. Have you forgotten that I know how much you enjoy sex? Me being pregnant shouldn't halt our spicy activities."

"Baby, you know I am a master at the right hand of the law!" Dayton exclaimed talking about the way he knows how to get himself off if he needed to.

"That's not the same and you know it. I love pleasing you."

Dayton leaned down and placed an openmouthed kiss on her neck. Kima slid around on the cold marble without pause. Under the hot skin of her behind, already steaming with need, it was the perfect combination.

"I love watching you pleasure yourself for me," he moaned against her sensitive skin.

"That is something we enjoy; watching each other," Kima added, with a nice, slow lick across both of her lips.

"You're right. There are a million ways we can love through anything. Are you sure you're okay this morning? Your hands are making things really, really hard for me, as I know you can tell."

Dayton was struggling to hold back when what he wanted to do was sink into Kima to the hilt. He was ready to hit her pleasure points again and again.

"Then love me and don't fight me on this. I need you right here," Kima said pointing to the area between her legs. To prove her point even more, she moistened the tips of two of her fingers and kept her eyes on Dayton as he followed the direction her fingers were going in.

When she swiped them across her already moist womanhood because he does that to her, she heard an animalistic groan come from him. She had him and she wanted him. Opening her legs wider and leaning back against the mirror, Kima slid her hips even closer to the edge. That was all Dayton would need and she knew it. His eyes darkened with a hazy, hooded look.

On cue and thankful that he was naked and Kima was too under her nighty, Dayton pulled her hips to him, leaned all the way forward to join their lips as he slid oh so gently into her waiting body, already moist and ready for him. On his first pass in, he was about to lose his mind and found he was already close to climaxing before her; a first for him. He'd never done that before. Kima's pleasure was always first, never his, unless that was her intention. There was something really different about being inside of her this morning.

"Kima – baby, you are really wet and it's driving me wild. Damn!" Dayton yelled as his body plunged forward, fast and hard. He had no control. He didn't want any even if he could muster it up. He could see Kima's full desire as her body pushed back against the mirror behind her. She looked so sexy in heat.

"I love you, Day," Kima moaned against his lips before pulling his head down into the area between her face and her shoulder.

Every part of her came alive as she matched him stroke for stroke; they were in rhythm with each other. She wanted to give him more, but she was limited by the way she was leaning back on the counter. Without regret, she let her legs be lifted high up and onto Dayton's shoulders on each side, as his powerful body moved into her with strong, piston-like strokes. She was in heaven. She was flying. Her body was on fire.

"Yes, yes, yesssss!" she yelled. "Don't you dare hold back. You can't hurt me or the baby. Give me you, Day – all of you!" she screamed. She hoped no one was outside just walking by. They would get an earful.

Dayton heard her plea and he followed her instructions.

He didn't know if he'd ever been this aroused before. Kima's body felt new. They had always been adventurous in the way and the places they made love. This position and the feel of her gripping him while the slippery sounds of their coming together sang to him with a sweet melody. He was in a joyous state of euphoria when Kima screamed out her release. He watched it slam into her again and again as her legs flailed about his shoulders. He felt the essence squirt from her body, drenching his legs. Her hips bucked into him as he pounded into her relentlessly. He couldn't stop even if he wanted to.

Placing his hands against the mirror he joined her in orgasmic bliss. His body bounded so freely as images spun around his head like a cartoon character with pictures of other characters circling around their heads. His last thought before he gave into the pleasure was that he knew he was having an out of body experience.

Dayton growled like a wild beast. He stretched his neck as high as he could as Kima's body claimed all of him. He could hear Kima's words of love, but even they sounded as if they were coming from a distance away.

Then it happened. Kima screamed again. She was having another orgasm. Dayton knew he dared not stop.

Kima didn't know what was happening to her. Her

body was on fire with need. The more Dayton gave her, the more she needed. Was it being pregnant that heightened her body's feelings and reactions to being sexually stimulated by him?

She tried to focus on using her body to bring him even more pleasure but while she was trying to do that, she could feel that twinge of desire between her legs, a sign that another release was about to hit her. She didn't have time to prepare herself when it happened. For a second, she thought she was about to strangle Dayton with her legs, not just on his shoulders anymore, but curved a little around his neck. Still, he didn't stop. His hips rocked into her and she took every single, delicious stroke. She peaked and let go with a groan that scared her. She reached and held onto his biceps and let their loving take her away to a place in her head where there was only her and Dayton. Their love for each other was that powerful.

As they slowed and Dayton's head rested against the mirror, neither of them spoke as their breathing slowed to a pace that would allow for words.

"Baby, if you were not already pregnant, you would be after that. What the hell did you do to me? I think your body had me under some kind of spell. I can barely feel my feet!" Dayton screamed jokingly.

"You? My legs up on your shoulders are numb, but in a good way," Kima declared.

"Shoot," Dayton professed and stepped back on wobbly legs to lower her legs, taking the time to massage each one. "I'm sorry about that. I don't know what came over me. I'm telling you, your body did something wild and crazy to me and I loved it!" he yelled, picking Kima up and taking her straight out of the bathroom and onto the bed.

"Okay, I know I said I wanted to go out today, but after that, I want to stay in and you stay with me. After a good nap, I'm going to need a repeat," Kima joked.

"Right. Neither one of us would survive. You be still while I get you a warm washcloth."

"Why don't we take a bath together and then we can get out of here. I want to go see your mother."

"Are you sure?" he asked, peaking from around the wall that led to the bathroom.

"I am. I want to see everyone, but mainly her. You have talked so lovingly about her since the moment we met. I want to thank her for you. I love you," she said right before a gigantic yawn escaped from her lips.

Dayton came back to the bed, leaned over the bed and kissed her passionately.

"I love you too. I'll run the bath. You rest for a bit."

Kima rolled over and tried to do that. For what seemed like a brief moment, she was able to forget about the outside world and how her father was out in it. It was time she focused. She had all of her mother's papers with her in Montana. She needed to start doing something for herself. She needed to find her father. His identity had to be somewhere in all of those papers. She was going to find out all she could in order to locate him. Oscar can't be the only family she has.

Curling her body around one of the pillows on the bed, Kima tried to fight the sleep that threatened her eye lids. Closing them, she rested her hand on her stomach and thought about the life they would have as Dayton loved them. This was family, she thought. What she had with Oscar as her father was anything but a family. It was far from love. It was evil. She needed more; she needed better. She needed to find her family. Those were her last thoughts before sleep won.

11

He wasn't leaving Bozeman. Oscar had decided that four days ago when he'd been tossed off of the Sullivan ranch as if he was a peasant. He wasn't going anywhere without Kima. He didn't care what anyone else said or thought on the matter. She was his daughter and he had every right to see her. Finding out from Dayton's family that she didn't want to see him was a humiliating moment for him. He was Oscar Tillery and no one talked to him or belittled him as Dayton's family had.

He paced around his hick-town hotel that didn't compare to the luxurious places he was used to staying in. After being thrown off the ranch and told to never return, not even for his daughter, he didn't know where to go. What he did know was his destination wouldn't be getting on a plane; at least not yet. He had to find a way to get through to Kima, whose cell phone had not been on since she'd last been in Australia.

Standing from the foot of the bed where he'd been sitting for the last hour, he looked out of the window of the hotel and down at the rental car he was able to get at the airport when he arrived, again, something way below his standards. He had to settle for what they had available. It was some white Toyota that made him stand out like a sore thumb. The town was so small that people looked his way knowing he was a stranger.

Now that he was in the United States, he would call his office back home and have better arrangements made for himself. His assistant, Erin, had made his flight arrangement to the U.S. which took him into Los Angeles. He originally thought that Kima may have traveled there to visit one of her friends who lived there. Being unable to locate her fueled his anger.

It all started when he arrived at the race track for the race the day she stopped by his house to tell him she was pregnant. He had been wrong to throw her out, but he was mad. Her continued disobedient behavior had reached its peak with him. Getting to the track, some of the men who worked for him warned him that there was an incident and he was being blamed for it. His first thought was that Dayton had been dealt with and he didn't have to wait for the race for that to happen. Then he saw Rusty coming toward him with a murderous look on his face. Luckily the men Oscar always had in place were there to protect him from whatever Rusty's intentions were. After a lot of back and forth, he was able to learn that not only was Dayton not going to race that day or any other day, but he was already headed out of Australia with Kima in tow.

By way of Rusty, he'd been called a menace, a peril,

a terrorist and every other defamatory description the burly yet fit manager could come up with. Rusty had his own men with him and the thugs Oscar was always able to scramble up didn't compare in size or strength to Rusty's men. He had no choice but to back down and go on a search for his daughter. If she thought she was getting away from him, she had another thing coming. What he couldn't figure out was how did Rusty find out that Dayton's car had been tampered with? Who spilled that information? There were only three people who knew about it and he couldn't imagine either man snitching. The men he kept around were loyal to him. Somehow, Rusty had found out and threatened legal action once he could prove it was him who was behind the sabotage attempt that would have caused Dayton his life.

Thinking back over the last few days of trying to find Kima, Oscar couldn't fathom why he hadn't thought of Dayton's hometown first. He knew about Dayton's family but hadn't spent a lot of time focusing on them. There was never a doubt that his family had money because the buy-in for the sponsorship of a driver alone ranged from five to ten million dollars for a Primary sponsor. That included logos around the hood and quarter panels of the cars along with signage below the quarter panels, most of the two posts, the equipment, the uniforms, as well as the color scheme of the car and team uniforms. Salaries of the pit crew were paid by the Sullivans, as well as their travel expenses. His team had major sponsorships from around the world, but Dayton brought in the most. There was still a long list of companies hoping to sponsor him and the team that he led, but Dayton was firm that his primary sponsor would be his family's ranch and all of its subsidiary businesses.

There were people who took care of that at TOBIT Motorsports. Details like that Oscar never had to focus too much attention on. He should have been paying more attention to the day-to-day operations, but his only concern was the financial side of it and how much he could line his pockets with before he was found out. There were people on his payroll at the company who helped him hide invoices and skim money in ways that were undetectable; at least he hoped so. It wasn't until Kima disappeared that he began asking questions about Dayton and his family. He knew of the Sullivan Ranch, but until he got to Bozeman and saw that name all over the place, he had no idea just how rich the family was.

On the plane ride, his fat fingers couldn't type fast enough as he found one article after the other on the family. He thought he was rich and that Andrew was rich, but neither of them compared to the kind of money the Sullivans had. He even found a story that had been done on Dayton about a year ago. He had been questioned about racing for a living when he didn't even need the money. It had been rumored that he was worth over thirty million dollars by himself.

That's not counting the wealth of his entire family. The more he read, the more he wondered if he was chasing the wrong family. Perhaps having Kima knocked up by Dayton was the better deal than the one he made with Andrew. The problem was that it seemed the Sulllivans were on the up-and-up with their business dealings. He couldn't find anything negative about them anywhere. Their empire was expanding so fast under the leadership of David Sullivan and his son Shelton that soon, the family would be one of the richest in the world. What he couldn't figure out was, with all of their wealth, why would they continue to settle for living in Bozeman, Montana? There were more well-appointed and financial equivalent places to plant roots, based on their wealth than on a ranch. His daughter being connected to them wasn't such a bad idea except for the fact that he was in deep with others who expected him and Kima to fall in line.

Oscar knew his first mistake was arriving at that ranch alone. He should have brought men with him, but he needed them in South America to deal with his other business. The few that were left had to stay with the racing circuit to keep an eye on his investments. He thought it would be easy to find Kima and drag her back to Australia to seal his deal with the Gaynor family. He should be calling them the Gaynor crime family with all the criminal business activities they were involved in. Still, this is where he was and he had to stay under the radar while here. He needed a plan.

First, he needed to return the calls his housekeeper had been making to him all morning.

"Edna? You've called ten times this morning," he said when she answered.

"Mr. Oscar, there are men here looking for you. I thought they were gone but they are sitting in cars waiting for you to return. They told me that I needed to find you. What should I do?" she asked.

Oscar's pressure shot up. He knew who they were and he was glad he wasn't at home. Besides dealing with Andrew and his demands all the time, he also had Carlos Cardoza with whom he had also cut a side deal with behind Andrew's back. With the shipment of cars from one country to another for races, there was also the inclusion of a huge shipment of drugs and Carlos was, no doubt, looking for his money. He had yet to pay him because he was looking at the money from Andrew to use to pay Carlos while also cutting the drugs to mix them with other drugs and chemicals to make them go a longer way for the money. He'd started having a team he recruited to do that. He had started making a fortune with that. What he hadn't planned on was his business dealings with any of them to be going this long. He couldn't deny that the money was good. The plan was to do it, cut and run. Greed took over and he owed more people than he wanted to, which meant he was losing a large share of his own money. He needed Kima to marry Nelson, thereby eventually selling her company to Andrew. That would get the man off of his back. Things were falling apart and now there were men at his house looking for him. Kima messed up everything.

"Do nothing, Edna. Maybe you should not be at the house for a while."

"But, but – where will I go? I live here. I don't have any place else to go."

He heard the fear in her voice but didn't care. He had his own issues to deal with.

"I pay you enough. Go to a hotel. Don't you have family?" he asked.

"No, sir. I come from Salvador. I have no one here but you and missy Kima."

"Edna, I can't help you. I have a lot going on. Stay at the house if you want. Those men aren't leaving. They are very dangerous. Do whatever. Don't call me again. They might find out and hurt you."

Oscar heard her about to say something else before he ended the call. He didn't care. Edna was a loose end anyway. He was wondering if she was the leak that told someone, perhaps Kima, about what he'd had done to Dayton's car. He couldn't trust anyone. He was on his own. Anyone could be bought, including those closest to him. He had to get Kima back on his own. That was the only way to settle the biggest score he had. With the money from that, he could pay his debts and disappear without having to look over his shoulder.

He knew she'd turned her phone off, but eventually, she would turn it back on. That was her only means of communicating with her friends. He decided to send her a text anyway. He was hoping she'd read it soon and respond. After all, he was still her father and the only family she had.

"Kima, you need to call me as soon as possible. Did you hear what your boyfriend's family did to me? First, they assaulted me and then they threatened me if I came back looking for you. We need to talk. I know we didn't leave things on a good note, but there is still time to fix all of this. I don't know what Dayton and his family have been filling your head with, but I did not try to hurt him. We are in danger if you don't marry Nelson. Think of yourself and that baby. Do the right thing and call me. It's dad."

He would give her a few days. She had to eventually come off that ranch and when she did, he would confront her. She had to know that if she wants to save Dayton, she would do as he asked. He wasn't the biggest fish that they had to worry about. Soon and very soon, Bozeman will have more visitors who were more deadly than he was. It was only a matter of time before they find him and then find her. He was hoping they would find her first. Kima was his daughter, but he would send her to the slaughter first if it meant protecting his own head. That's just the way things were.

Needing a shower and a plan, he opened the duffle bag of clothes he brought with him. If he was doomed to stay in this town for the foreseeable future, he may as well see what it had to offer. Hopefully, there were women who didn't mind entertaining a stranger. The other bag of money he brought with him on his private flight from Australia to California and then from there to here, he knew he would be able to buy just about anyone, especially a woman in need. They were everywhere.

Oscar smiled at himself as he walked past the mirror. He didn't doubt that things would work out. He always came out on top. This time would be no different. It was all up to Kima. She had to decide if she wanted to see her baby be born. She would follow his way of thinking if she wanted to make sure Dayton lived long enough to see his child being born. He didn't care. He only cared about her financial worth. Her worth was the same dead or alive.

12

Kima was holding onto Dayton's hand so tight that when he winced from the pain of her crushing his knuckles together, she giggled and apologized. She then grabbed onto the fabric of his green t-shirt, the first piece of fabric she could feel. When he patted her hand, she knew that he was trying to help calm her down.

"Sorry. I'm nervous. It's been a few days and I'm finally meeting your mother and father. Are you sure they don't hate me for bringing drama to their home?" she asked.

Dayton smiled down at her as they walked from his truck to the front steps.

After another day of not venturing out, Kima woke before him this morning and quickly showered. She rushed to get dressed in a pair of denims that, thankfully, still fit. She added a crisp white t-shirt and matching white sneakers. She pulled her hair up into a tight bun and added light makeup. She needed it after days of not letting the sun meet her face. When Dayton woke, after being out late the night before with his brothers, she was ready for him.

After making love the day before in the tub and then that afternoon in the bed, she'd slept in until he showed up with a late lunch and then dinner sent over by his mother. What she found special was that Dayton must have told her about the morning nausea she continued to experience. She sent over a remedy that Kima needed to drink as soon as she woke up in the morning. She was hesitant at first, but Dayton told her that it was full of vitamins and other natural remedies. There was nothing that would hurt the baby in it. In fact, his mother believed the baby would love it. First thing this morning when she rose, she drank the full glass he'd placed next to the bed. She laid awake and waited, anticipating the meal from the night before would provide business as usual with the porcelain throne in the bathroom. She waited and waited and nothing happened. There was no nausea, no throwing up or anything even close to that. She felt amazing. Still, she was cautious as she showered and got dressed. Even Dayton couldn't believe when he woke that she hadn't felt the need to toss her stomach.

His mother is amazing. She had even asked Dayton if his mother was thinking of bottling up and selling that stuff to women around the world who, like her, experienced terrible morning sickness. He said he didn't know, but suggested that maybe that would be something she and his mother could talk about to help tamper down her nervousness.

She waited for him to get dressed and now, here they were approaching the house.

"Don't be sorry. Just so you know, my mother doesn't have a hateful bone in her body unless someone comes for one of us. I love you and so will she. Trust me. Ready?" he asked her.

Even though she was worried, she still hadn't felt the pang of morning sickness. Her stomach was still good, though she was starving. When Dayton called his mother to say they were coming over, she told him that she was having Sarah prepare a feast for them. Him joining them was not just for Kima's benefit but also because Sarah made the best pancakes from scratch. Her fried potatoes and onions were mouth-watering.

Opening the outside door because the inside door was already opened with the most wonderful smell coming through it, Dayton stood back and made room for Kima to enter first. She looked around and couldn't believe her eyes. From the outside, the house was made of wood and brick and was a two-level gorgeous structure. Dayton told her that over the past few years, there had been major additions added and now the house was almost seven thousand square feet. From the outside it was huge and the inside was immaculate. She didn't expect the house to be so breathtaking.

When they pulled up, she saw wood wraparound porches on both levels, with a massive deck above the front entrance. Dayton had noted that his parents' bedroom led out to that deck where it overlooked a spectacular view of the mountains. Dayton mentioned that in all of their houses, the bedrooms faced mountains. Inside, she saw vaulted ceilings and two winding staircases with large oversized windows in every room. The house was full of light and the size of the rooms were the size of her entire flat in Australia. To her right, she saw a large family room equipped with a wall size television, probably eighty inches or more. She saw the most inviting sectional in mint green, one of her favorite colors.

Kima marveled at everything she saw as she followed Dayton toward the smells of breakfast cooking.

"Mom?" he yelled.

Kima's uneasiness leaped to a whole new level when a woman, who looked to be a lot younger than she imagined of someone who had five adult children, came around a bend and greeted them. Kima waited as Dayton kissed his mother on both of her cheeks before turning around.

"Ma, this is Kima McDonald. Kima, this is my mother, Marta Sullivan."

"It's nice to meet you, ma'am," Kima said and extended her hand even as it shook from anxiety.

"Come give me a hug, dear. We don't shake hands around here. You certainly are beautiful. You could use a few extra meals with that baby and all."

Kima relished in the tight hug. She was

embarrassed when she held on a little longer than she should have. His mother made her remember the loving hugs her own mother used to give her; a mother she missed more and more every day, especially with the baby coming.

"Sorry for holding on so long," she stated softly.

"No problem at all. My children know a hug is an easy thing to get from me, so anytime you need or want one, you come and get it!" Marta exclaimed. "Sarah? Come see who's here," she yelled.

Within seconds, another woman came bounding out from the back of the house. Kima found herself, once again, pulled into a loving hug. She was already loving being here on the ranch. She immediately thought about Edna, who was the only person who still hugged her like this. She missed Edna more than she missed anyone else. She wondered how she was faring back home.

"Welcome to the Sullivan Ranch, Kima!" Sarah exclaimed.

"Thank you. It's so gorgeous here. This house is so gorgeous. Dayton's description didn't do it justice," Kima said looking around.

"I tried," he said and hunched his shoulders.

"He can give you a tour after you eat something. Sarah is the best cook in the world. There are pancakes, which you will see Dayton embarrass himself by gulping them down. There are also eggs scrambled or she can make you an omelet. We have bacon, sausage, ham slices, fried potatoes with onions and peppers, grits, Danish, which she bakes fresh here on the ranch and a ton of other things including lots of fruit."

"Wow, that's a lot. Thanks for sending over food everyday along with the large baskets of fresh fruit and breads. I guess Dayton told you how much I love fruit."

"That he did. He also mentioned you loved banana bread, so Sarah will keep some of that fresh for you each day."

"You kids wash up and come sit," Sarah said, pointing toward the large wooden kitchen table with enough seats, Kima could tell, that could seat Dayton's entire family.

"There is a washroom right off the kitchen," Marta pointed. "Dayton can show you. How are you feeling this morning?" she added.

"Oh, I feel wonderful. Thanks for sending the drink over. It worked. Today was the first morning in a few weeks that I haven't been sick right after waking."

"Well, you'll have that every morning. I've had enough of it made to stock up the fridge at your house. Until the feelings subside, let me know if you start to run out. One small glassful each morning will do the trick. Just make sure it's room temperature."

Kima nodded and rushed to the washroom. When she returned to the kitchen, there were two other women there. She recognized Brielle from the night that Oscar had arrived. She had come by the house with Dayton. There were also pictures Dayton carried around with him of his family. The other woman she remembered but didn't quite place the name.

"Hello," Kima smiled.

"You're up and moving about. It's about time. I thought my brother was never going to let you out of that house. He wouldn't even let me visit," Brielle said, pulling her into a hug. A hugging family; Kima loved everything about it.

"Well, don't blame him for all of it. So much has happened and for some reason, this baby only wants me to eat and sleep. I've never had this much rest," Kima said.

"I blame Day for everything; he knows that," Brielle exclaimed before smacking Dayton lightly on the back of the head where he already sat at the table. When she went into the washroom, he went off to the bathroom that was off the family room.

"How are you feeling?" Brielle asked, sitting next to where Kima sat, across from Dayton, who was already shoveling food in his mouth as if he were starving.

"Really, Day? You are not Tarzan who lived in the woods. We weren't taught to eat like animals either. You can use a fork and knife," Brielle joked.

"Girl, do you have any idea how long it's been since I've had a full spread in front of me like this of Sarah's cooking? I'm going to eat it anyway I want!" Dayton joked and rolled his eyes.

Kima listened to their exchange and laughed as they shared crazy facial features across the table.

"I'm Gizelle," the other woman said.

"Perry's wife, right?" Kima asked.

"Yes. Marta texted that you would be here for breakfast. I thought I would come eat with you and welcome you to the ranch," Gizelle said.

"Thank you for that. Everyone is so nice," Kima acknowledged.

"Well, Day can be grumpy, but the rest of us are always nice," Brielle chimed in.

"Don't let me start in on the beast within when you're mad at the world!" Dayton exclaimed.

"Kima, pay them no mind. Brielle and Dayton are like this whenever they are in the same room. That's their way of saying they miss each other when Dayton is on the circuit. Go ahead and fix what you want on your plate," Marta said.

Kima looked down at the table where the food sat on a circular device that when moved with your hands, all of the food would eventually come your way. She guessed that was needed for a family as large as theirs.

"This is a lot of food. Do you cook like this all the time and for everyone on the ranch?" Kima asked Sarah.

"I always cook for the family here in the house and the kids and their families. I've been doing that since the birth of the first Sullivan child. I have a staff of forty who assists with providing food for this side of the ranch where the daycare and school are, as well as the ranch hands who live and work here on the ranch."

"You won't find better or tastier food anywhere. Sarah has been feeding us like this since we were babies. It looks filling and heavy, but she uses a lot of natural ingredients in her meals. She can make you anything you want. Know that she'll also keep the refrigerator stocked at the house now that Dayton is back and you're growing my little niece or nephew. I swear this family is on the ball with procreating!" Brielle shouted.

"As long as it's not you," Dayton retorted quickly.

"Enough. Let Kima eat in peace," Marta asserted.

"Have you met anyone else?" Gizelle asked.

"Not yet. Now that I'm feeling better, I hope to meet everyone," Kima responded.

"Parker and Nick aren't here. They finally left for their honeymoon last night. With all of the excitement, they postponed leaving for a few days. Nick wanted to be sure things had settled before he left. My kids are in school, so you'll meet them later, perhaps," Gizelle answered.

"How old are your kids?"

"I have a son, Brody, who just turned four and Carrie is now five."

"I guess you know Dayton and I are expecting," Kima shared.

"Yes. Congratulations. How far along are you?" Gizelle asked.

"Two months and a week or so."

"I'm pregnant too," Gizelle added.

"Something I just found out. I love the idea of all of these babies on the ranch," Marta added.

"Oh, congratulations to you too," Kima said to Gizelle.

"Mom, Kima needs a doctor while she's here. Can you help with that?" Dayton asked.

"Of course. We have a few doctors here on the ranch, but not really an OB, which is what she needs. I'll speak to the doc and get a recommendation. Gizelle, what about your doctor?" Marta asked.

"Definitely. Kima and I can call her after breakfast. You will love her."

"Thank you," Kima replied.

"I have to run out. Kima, you're good?" Dayton asked.

"Of course, she's good, fool! What are we, chopped liver? I got this. If you have to leave, just leave. Why must you announce your every move. You still do that? I'm going to show Kima around, if she's up for that. I also want to get some dirt on you to throw in your face at random. I bet Kima has some good stories," Brielle shouted out.

Dayton stood.

"Whatever. Kima loves me. She isn't going to tell you any secrets."

"I don't know, Dayton. If Brielle passes me that plate of ham so that I can get another slice, I may be persuaded!" Kima joked.

"Baby? You'd sell me out for some food!" Dayton

yelled.

"This baby sure would!" she kidded.

Dayton kissed her on the lips and hugged his mother.

"I'm supposed to meet Shelton to go horseback riding. I'll be back later. I have my cell if anyone needs me."

"She'll be fine, Day, go," Marta said. "I don't want to hear anything about horse racing. Your love for speed still itches my spirit."

"I know, Ma, and I promise to be careful. I have every plan to be here for Kima and my baby. Love you all!" Dayton screamed as he raced for the front door.

"That boy is always in a rush," Sarah said.

"Always," Brielle added.

Kima didn't weigh in. She was imagining ways where Dayton was not in a rush; in a way she dared not share with his family.

Kima watched Marta take the seat that Dayton had abandoned, moving his now empty plate to the side.

"I look forward to us getting to know each other. My son loves you and that matters to me. Before you question being here on the ranch and what that means, it means you're family. If there is anything you need, all you have to do is ask any of us. We're here for you. You're going through a lot, but us Sullivans stick together. Let me tell you all about me, dear, and before we get up from this table, you'll feel like you've known us all your life," Marta said.

Kima smiled when she wanted to cry. The warm welcoming gave her a greater sense of family. It also reminded her that she had a family out there somewhere that wasn't Oscar. She couldn't wait to find them with the hope that they would be as welcoming as the Sullivans.

13

Dayton, Perry, Shelton and David stood at the entrance
to the large metal fence that surrounded the fifty-five-
acre property that would soon be the Sullivan Raceway.
Dayton couldn't believe what he was seeing. As a kid,
he dreamed of this day. With the help and support of
his family, they were making it happen for hm.

"What do you think, Day? I know we can't see it all
from here, because it will be a mile long track, but you
get the size of it," Shelton asked.

He was the family money person who kept them in
the green and had their wealth multiplying on a daily
basis.

"It's massive. After hanging out with you last night
and going over everything, I can say that you planned
for all of my questions. I'm glad we're using this part of
the land where we didn't have to cut down many trees,"
Dayton said.

He let his eyes take in the massive sight before him
of land he played on as a kid. There were many days of
racing dirt bikes with his brothers and their friends

along with riding their ATVs across the mostly grassy and mountainous region.

"This was the old Baker property. Once Paul Baker died, his kids didn't want anything to do with ranch life. It seems, old man Baker left in his will that if the kids didn't want the land, that they were to offer it to us first. He knew Pop would do something great with it. In fact, they reached out to us three years ago and it's taken this long to finally acquire it with a lot of negotiating," Shelton noted.

"How many acres did they have?" Dayton asked.

"Seventy-four acres. We acquired all of it. Pop hasn't decided what we'd like to do with the rest of it, just yet. Because it's so close to the track and we want to stay up with what's popular with the culture that would bring in major income, we were thinking about a large concert venue with indoor and outdoor space for concerts. That would also bring in a huge revenue for the hotels on the other quarter of the property when you look at it in four sections," Shelton said.

"Big plan after big plan," Perry acknowledged. "This has been the plan for many years."

"I'm glad you boys see the vision. I know there are a lot of things we can do with the wealth we have accumulated. I always want to think about people and how we can bring them together in a world that still rages with hate," David said.

"True. Also add into that the number of jobs we have created in the past few years. There are people who never thought about living here who are moving here simply because of the increasing number of good paying jobs we offer all over the ranch. With Shelton's construction company growing by leaps and bounds, he's added three hundred workers on in the past month just to begin the work on this track," David added.

"Who knew we had this in us," Shelton said.

"I did. I always knew," David replied quickly.

"Yeah. I remember us being kids and you telling us the stories of what you wanted the ranch to be. To see it come to fruition is incredible. How could I not want to be on the ranch?" Dayton asked and then regretted the words he'd spoken out loud.

For days now, he'd been thinking that to himself, but not actually stating it where someone could hear him.

"Day, this is home; this is home, son. You have a right to live here or anywhere else. You have always wanted to see the world beyond what the ranch was. You and Nick have always been like that. Your mom and I never pushed for any of you to make your life here, but it would always be an option if that's what you wanted. Are you having any change of heart about racing?" David asked.

Dayton looked to his brothers and his father as they waited his response. He'd been thinking about a lot lately, especially now that all of his decisions needed to include Kima and the baby. He loved racing, but the love he once had for being all over the world and behind the wheel of his prized cars no longer held the love they once had. His priorities were changing. He once thought he was on the right track to the life he wanted, but that track was different now. It included a woman he loved more than anything. He had a baby that he couldn't wait to hold in his arms. He has changed just as his life is changing; so, has his dreams.

He turned and faced them where they each now leaned back against the fence.

"We're about to have company," Dayton noted as a group of men in trucks headed their way.

"They're a part of the security team who will guard this land around the clock until the construction is done. We'll probably get them under contract for the security of the venue once it's built. These guys don't play. I told them we were coming and they're coming to open the gate," Shelton said.

"Cool. Back to Pop's question, I still love racing. I think it will always be in my blood, but I don't love it as much as I love Kima. I discovered what I thought would never happen to me; I am willingly giving her my heart. We are trying to build a life together and yes, I want that life to be here on the ranch. I need to talk to Kima more about that, but when I found out I was having a baby, I imagined my son or daughter roaming the many hills, lakes, valleys and trenches that made up our lives here as we were growing up. I had the best childhood right here on this ranch. I think somewhere in me chasing the fastest car, I forgot about that life. I want my child to have that, too. I don't think convincing Kima will be the problem. The issue is going to be her father. Whatever he is wrapped up in is going to keep visiting Kima wherever she is. I didn't realize how treacherous he was until Kima told Rusty about my car and the danger of it all. There are also some other things that she's become aware of that has us at a loss."

"Oh, what's that?" Perry asked. "You know we can handle anything when we do it together. You know what I went through with Gizelle's ex-husband and what he tried to do to her. I would give my life for her and the kids just as I know you would for Kima and your baby. Hell, I almost did. I was wailing on him with so much force after he tried to kill Gizelle, that I didn't care if I took the breath from his body. My love had me out of control at the thought of what he could have done to her if we hadn't found her. That's the way we love our women. I don't want you taking any risks, Day. If we put our heads together and put the full force of our resources behind a resolution, we'll figure this out. We got this," Perry added.

"Thanks, Bro. Kima has been going through some papers she brought with her. She's mad that she left so many at her father's house. There could be information that proves her father had her mother and her mother's lawyer killed. It seems that Oscar also may have the information that could lead Kima to her biological father, something her mother would never share with her in order to keep him and his family safe from Oscar. Her stepdad is a vindictive man, as I've come to learn," Dayton said.

"I think it's time we looked a little deeper into Oscar Tillery. We need to know more about who we're dealing with," David said.

"I'll get my guys from the private investigation firm we use often to do some checking. Those guys can literally find a needle in a haystack. They turn over every stone to find what they need. In the meantime, so you all know, Oscar is still in town. Perry, you want to tell them what you told me?" Shelton asked.

"Damn!" Dayton shouted. "Sorry, Pop," he said looking to his father who patted him on the shoulder letting him know he understood his frustration.

"Yeah. I was hanging out with Marcus two nights ago, talking about how the Sullivans can sponsor the new little league football and baseball teams that the Sheriff's office is kicking off later this year. We were having steaks at our favorite watering hole when in walks Oscar. This man has some nerve. I stayed out of sight as not to cause a ruckus in the bar. Marcus was in plain clothes. It seems that Oscar loves to party. He flirted with everything in a skirt. He also tossed back quite a few. I was hoping he would try to hop in his car and drive at the end of the night so that Marcus could pick him up, but he didn't. He let the bartender call him a ride back to his hotel. I filled Marcus in as we followed him in my truck to see where he was staying. It seems, he's at a hotel right at the airport. I don't think he's leaving anytime soon. In fact, he looked like he was making himself right at home here in Bozeman," Perry explained.

"We're going to have to deal with him, now!" Dayton shouted. "Kima can't live as a prisoner on the ranch just to be protected from him. She won't want that and neither do I. I want her to love being in Bozeman, not fear life here," he added.

"I'm ahead of you, Day, so don't worry. Marcus is the Sheriff and he knows what's going on. He has four new Deputy Sheriff's he just hired to add to his current team with all of the new folks moving to this area. Marcus' ex-wife is in real estate. He said she can barely keep up with the number of house sales she's been getting from the company she works for. I want to let him and his team deal with any legal issues with Oscar. Let him do what he does. You know how far we go back as kids, so he'd looking out for us. Now that he knows where Oscar is and what he looks like, he's making his team aware," Perry clarified.

"I may stop in and pay Marcus a visit to stay on top of this, too," Shelton added.

"Marcus is heading out on vacation in a few days, so you'll probably end up with one of his Deputy Sheriff's," Perry said.

"Speaking of vacation, did I hear that Brielle is heading out of town on vacation?" Shelton asked.

"Yeah. It was sort of at the last minute. She never

takes time off," Perry explained.

"Who is she going with? I know she's not going alone?" David asked.

Each brother looked at him and knew the Papa Bear in him was about to rear its ugly head. They could all be that way with Brielle, but their father was worse.

"She's going with some friends who work at the amusement park here. They're going to Punta Cana in the Dominican Republic. She knows to stay in contact whenever she is off of the ranch," Perry said.

"Hearing Marcus is taking a vacation made me think of that group text Brielle sent out about her trip. Anyway, I'll stop and see one of the Sheriff Deputies," Shelton said.

"I hear one is a cutie. I think her name is McKenna Gibson," Perry noted.

This time all heads turned to Shelton."

"What?" Shelton asked and smiled. He didn't want to admit that he already knew about her and was looking forward to saying hello. He noticed the other day how sexy the new Deputy Sheriff looked in her uniform. He could imagine what she would look like out of it.

"You know what," Perry added.

"Can we *not* get into my personal life right now. Y'all out here covering the market on falling in love. I still have a black heart when it comes to love. I'm too busy sampling the luscious..."

Shelton started to say more and then remembered

his father was with them. He was sure he'd heard enough about his son's life while living in the city.

Dayton laughed out loud.

"Go ahead and finish. I want to hear all about it. Besides, I need a little longer of seeing you in jeans and cowboy boots. I can't remember the last time I didn't see you in a designer suit and shades, all cool, calm and suave for the ladies!" Dayton said. "You even came dressed like that to one of my recent races. When you show up, they ladies claw to get at you," Dayton added.

"Yeah, take it all in. I'll be back in my suit minutes after I take my horse back. If it wasn't for how my legs looked in jeans, I wouldn't wear them. Y'all hear the whispers about me and jeans. The ladies prefer me in suits – or out of them," Shelton said.

"Ego much?" Perry asked, jokingly.

"Okay, enough of this. I've spent years keeping all of your escapades away from your mother's ears and eyes. Shelton, don't you mess over that Deputy Sheriff. She just got here," David said.

"I hear you, Pop. Perry started it," Shelton chuckled.

"You'll let us know about anything they find, right?" Dayton inquired of Shelton.

He may be the youngest and he knows, his brothers often try to shield him from things, but this was his life and that of his family. He wouldn't be left out of what's happening.

"You will know what I know and when I know it.

Perry, you're leading the effort with the track here, so you need to focus on that. I have my team dealing with company business, so I have a little extra free time right now. I'm on it," Shelton assured them.

"So, you're possibly going to stay?" Perry asked Dayton.

"I can run the track and the team from here in Bozeman. I can even race on my own raceway and on my own circuit. I would also like to oversee the go-kart business," Dayton said.

"You're sure that will be enough for you?" David asked.

"Pop, we will own our own track. In fact, I need to work on getting my cars here. One is in North Carolina, two are in Canada and two are in Australia. The newest one isn't complete yet, but that can be brought here since the garage will be completed here on the ranch before anything else will. I plan to be hands-on with the building of all the cars from the business I know we'll get. The new thing are these E-cars. I've been learning more and more about them as my own car was being built. It's the future and we'll be at the precipice of that new way of racing. First and foremost, I need Oscar out of our lives and I need to figure out, if Kima agrees to stay, how to make that happen. She's not a U.S. citizen. I want my cars brought here, since the ranch owns them all. Before I forget, I need to figure out how to get all of Kima's things to this country along with more boxes of her mother's things that she left behind. Last night, Kima mentioned that the widow of her mother's attorney may have some files she could use as well," Dayton said.

"Let me work on those boxes from the lawyer's family. I can have my attorney reach to the family," Shelton said. "I'll also see what the private agency I talked about can help with, including finding out how we can work on Kima's citizenship," Shelton said.

"Besides marrying her, which I plan to do?" Dayton said, surprising them all. He knew he had by the stunned looks staring back at him.

"What is it about the men in this family? I guess this is the season for weddings and babies. My how life has changed for us in a few short years!" David declared. "Your mother is already walking around on cloud nine. Wait until she hears this."

David motioned for them all to head to the entrance to the property so that they could get a better look at the entire acreage.

"Come on, let's hop back on the horses and go further in," David said. "I'll let you boys talk about how to help Dayton a little later. If you need me for anything, you know what to do. Just in case I don't say it often enough, I'm proud of each and every one of you. I love you very much. Keep doing the right things for yourselves and for the women in your lives."

When all eyes turned to Shelton, who was the only single one in the crew, Dayton laughed when Shelton walked away, not addressing what he knew the stares mean.

"Don't even think about it," he yelled over his shoulder.

"That's what we all said," Perry said, getting back up on the horse he'd rode out on.

"I'm the only one still saying it. Whatever has bitten all of you, I'm got some spray to prevent it happening to me. It's called, don't love them, just date them," he chuckled.

As they all mounted their horses as the gates were opened to let them in, Dayton thought about how good it felt to be back home and having Kima with him. Like Shelton, he declared his own forever kind of bachelorhood, but now, all he wanted was to marry Kima and make them a real family. He wanted her to be a Sullivan and to know that she would never need to have a man like Oscar around to call family. His actions were not that of a man who loved his daughter. Along with Shelton and any help he could give, he was looking forward to getting Oscar out of their lives for good.

Knowing Kima was safe with his mother, sister and sister-in-law smothering her with genuine kindness, Dayton rode his horse through the gate. When the need for speed overtook him, he raced the horse faster and heard the hooves of the horses behind him as his father and brothers attempted to catch up. This was the life, he thought as the fresh Bozeman air flew all around him.

14

Kima finally turned her cell phone back on, a month after her father first arrived in Bozeman. She was happy that, as far as she knew, he had not tried to come back onto the ranch to get her since that first night. She didn't turn it on to hear from him, but to let her friends know that she was alright. She knew that Nala and Bridget had to be worried sick about her. The story of Dayton's car being sabotaged at the last race in Australia had finally hit the national news, making its way to the United States. Mentioned in the news story was the possibility that her father had been involved someone.

While she and Dayton had taken off to Bozeman, Rusty had stayed behind to protect Dayton's cars until they were shipped out, which had just happened. Dayton woke up to a text that his cars were on their way. It took that much time to make it happen. Knowing anything could have happened to the cars, his family had sent a security team to all three locations where his cars were kept that would watch over them until they were brought to the ranch. Even with that, a team was in place to inspect each car before it was brought to a newly constructed hangar located on the ranch. It was located near where the new track construction had begun a few days ago. She had been ecstatic the day Dayton took her to let her see what their future would be.

"I could hear all that pinging from the shower. You finally decided to turn it on?" Dayton asked, surprising her with his presence. She'd been thinking about all that had gone on over the past month and didn't hear him walk in. She still wasn't listening when he entered their room with only a towel around his waist. When her eyes took in the muscly mountains of his body, she licked her lips at the thought of what she'd like to be doing. There was something about being pregnant that had her ready for him anytime her eyes saw him or her ears heard him. There was a time when they first met that she worried she couldn't keep up with his sexual prowess. His appetite was ravenous. There was never anything dull about how intentional he was about their pleasure. Since getting pregnant, all she can think of is feeding the potent state of arousal for him that she always seemed to be experiencing.

"Um," she said, trying to remember what his question was. Then she smiled with only her eyes and he knew.

"No, Kima. I just showered and you're already dressed," he laughed, shaking his head at how the tables have turned between them.

Though Dayton still desired her, he also knew that at any time, she would reach for him, even when he was asleep because her body was on fire for release. He always catered to her need for him. There were many nights, in the wee hours where she would wake up needing to feel him. Though he would be sound asleep, he would awaken the moment she dipped her head beneath the comforter. The party was on the minute she slipped his shaft into her mouth, already hard in anticipation of what he knew she could do with it. He was happily whipped!

Kima knew what she wanted. The idea was on her mind right now. As much pleasure as she knew her mouth could give to him, she got just as much pleasure out of watching him come apart knowing how much he loved oral sex; so did she.

"No, what?" she said slyly, reaching for the towel. When Dayton playfully moved out of her reach, she was then able to catch his arm and pull him back to her. Tossing her phone to the bed, not caring who had reached out to her, she only wanted Dayton.

"I know that look. I've seen it a lot lately," he said.

"And you love it each and every time. You should you would never deny me anything. All I had to do is ask."

"Baby, we were not talking about this when I said that."

When Dayton teased her and grabbed himself,

showing her that he was as much in need for her as she was for him, she pouted when he moved further away, slipping out of her grasp.

"We seem to be rushing by each other lately. I've been busy working with your mother in the office. I love it. She's had me sitting in on the meetings about branding and selling her cure for morning sickness. When I asked her about that, she told me I could be in on the early workings of getting it out to the public. That has kept me busy this past month along with thinking about school and if I'll be able to go to a college here. I'm not an American, yet."

"Yes, you'll be able to do that. I love that you enjoy working with my mother and being busy. I haven't felt so bad about spending all of my time on the plans for the track. Now, I'm finding I may be neglecting you and I never want that," Dayton explained.

"I just wanted to touch you; feel you; love on you the way you enjoy loving on me. I get so much out of pleasuring you. I didn't want you to think I meant you have been neglecting me. Last night, you beat me to bed. I was trying to get in a few last minutes with Brielle now that's she back. I couldn't wait to hear about her trip. Right now, I'm just missing you," Kima said softly.

Kima wouldn't reveal a secret that Brielle told her about her trip to Punta Cana. She didn't really go with friends. The sisterhood that they had achieved meant keeping her sister's secret until she was ready to tell everyone. Today, her thoughts were all on Dayton and what she wanted to do to him.

Kima's words stopped Dayton in his tracks before he was able to grab his shaving kit. She was right. There was a lot of activity around the ranch for the both of them. Not once did you realize that his desire to build their life on the ranch would make her feel lonely. He never wanted that.

"I'm sorry. I guess we have been operating on roller skates since we arrived, or at least I have."

"I'm not being unappreciative of what you're doing for us. I didn't hesitate when you asked me to stay here with you. I don't want to be anywhere else, but with you and our baby, who seems to really be growing at an expeditious rate these days. I love it here on the ranch. I love everything about being here. I just want a little more of you, like right now. We're rushing off, you to the hangar to get ready for your cars and me to the event center offices."

Dayton walked back over to Kima and stood in front of her, lifting her head to meet his gaze.

"There will never be a time that anything is more important than you. I agree, your belly is really poking out. When is your appointment for the sonogram?" he asked.

"In three days. I met Gizelle's doctor. She did an exam and told me to come for the sonogram in a few days. She's a wonderful woman and pretty young to be an OB. She wants me to come into her office. She doesn't use the medical facilities here on the ranch."

"Okay, I'm going with you."

"I thought that you would be busy. Gizelle offered to go with me since she has the day off from the school at the end of the week."

"Baby, I don't want you going to that appointment without me. I want to be there for everything."

Kima turned her head and looked at Dayton with a side-eye.

"Are you doing this because you think it's not safe for me to be off the ranch? Gizelle told me what happened to her when she decided to leave the ranch to help a friend thinking that her ex-husband was far away and not after her anymore. Do you think my father is still around?"

"No. He did return to Australia weeks ago. Shelton's guys were able to find that out. I don't think he has anyone here. Once, he was spotted riding by the ranch and Marcus, the Sheriff and close friend of our family had someone keeping an eye on him. They approached him the moment he turned onto the main road where the only thing on it is the ranch. He was given a warning to stay away. He told Marcus he's been trying to contact you."

"I wonder what finally made him leave. Do you know? I know you and your brothers have been handling things. I just wish you would keep me in the loop. I need to know, Dayton."

Hearing Kima's firm voice was all Dayton needed to hear.

"He got in a little trouble with a woman about three weeks ago. After spending the night in jail, he was threatened with further charges if he didn't leave. Marcus also shared with him that they knew of the suspicions around him when it came to what happened to Dayton's car. Suffice it to say, he didn't want any trouble. He finally realized you were not going back with him, nor were you going to marry Nelson. He took off for Australia but I hear he's not there anymore. There are people on the hunt for him. It seems he's gone into hiding someplace."

"Probably in Spain. That's where he's originally from and he has a lot of people there. He could definitely get lost in the crowd. See, there is no reason for you to worry about me."

Dayton cupped her face and kissed her lips.

"I still want to go to your appointment. I want to be there for every appointment."

"Okay. I didn't want you to hear about my weight gain. I can't fit anything anymore. I'm only a little over three months, if the calculation is right. We'll know tomorrow. Now, as for today..."

Kima let her actions speak in place of her words. She kept her eyes on his as she loosened the towel around his waist, smiling like a kid at Christmas when it fell in a heap around his feet as his penis jutted straight out at her as if it were calling her name, letting her know it was all for her. Without second guessing herself, she looked up, around his hard, thick, throbbing flesh and caught Dayton's eyes just as she gave the large tip of him a sweet, seductive kiss; not forgetting to add a little tongue to the action. She knew it would drive him crazy. When he sort of stumbled, she couldn't help the way she grinned with her own tongue now captured between her teeth.

"You know what? You are going to kill me. The woman I love is trying to put me in an early grave. I'm about to burst at the seams here," he quipped.

"Burst. Mmm, that's one of my favorite words."

Prolonging the agony, Kima teased him the way he enjoyed teasing her. It was their thing. It kept their love and their sex exciting.

Leaning forward again, this time, she let the now glistening tip of him rest in the opening of her buttoned top where her deep cleavage smiled out at him. Another thing being pregnant brought her was even bigger breasts, as if her 38DDs needed any more growth. To feed her baby one day, she would take them. For Dayton to feast on now, yes, she would take that too.

This time, with her tongue, she swiped it from the tip, all the way down, grasping his hardness in one hand. With the other, she reached below to stroke and massage the most sensitive part of his body. Thankfully, there was a dark brown dresser behind him that he could brace his hands on. When his legs quivered and he groaned out his pleasure Kima didn't stop. Loosening the buttons of her shirt with one hand and releasing the front clasp of her bra, she saw how happy that action made Dayton. She knew it was time to go for the gusto.

Taking him into her hands because both would be needed in order to encircle his full girth, Kima opened her mouth as wide as she could and took in as much of him as she could take. That got a shout of her name emitting from his mouth. As good as she knew her mouth felt to him, her body was on the brink of a release without his hands anywhere on him. For women who didn't get a rise out of pleasuring a man like this to the point of climaxing herself without being touched, had no clue what she was missing. This had never happened to her before; only with Dayton. They were that connected.

With her mouth, she moved over him, around him and delighted when his hand moved her hair out of the way as she worked so that he could see her face. Her head bobbing back and forth, his hips moving back in forth as the fingers of one hand now gripped her hair with the perfect amount of pressure, while the other grabbed as much of her breasts that could fill his hands. She suckled and licked and suckled even more, sucking the air out of her mouth as she let go more of him. When his hips began to piston lightly, she knew he was close. She held onto him tight when in the past, she would let go as his essence ejected from him. Not today. She was loving the feel of all of him in her mouth. They were one at this very moment and nothing was going to break that; definitely not when she knew he was on the brink; Dayton was so close. She knew his look. She could see him even while he rode in and out of her mouth. She increased the pressure of her hands moving up and down, moving them in a circular motion. The pressure, the suction, all together and in the next second, it started.

"Kima, no. Let go, baby. Kima!" Dayton yelled as he clinched his jaw tight. He knew what was coming; Kima did too and wouldn't turn him loose.

Kima ignored him. She held him in her grip and worked her mouth like never before.

Dayton let go of her hair, gripped the dresser behind him and roared like a lion. She'd never heard that kind of sound out of him before as she kept her mouth in place, taking all that he had to give and then more. Watching Dayton come apart like this and knowing that she did this to him and for was the kind of attention she never wanted to stop giving him.

Knowing he was spent and could barely stand, Kima finally turned his still hardened flesh loose, wiped her lips with her finger tips and smiled like a pro. For him, she would be his pro anything at any time. They both may get busy today, but neither will forget this very moment.

"Tasty," she gloated when Dayton's breathing turned to normal.

"Yup, I'm dying. I am and it's your fault. You've never done that before," he slurred. Dayton was still struggling to speak. His entire body was ablaze with awareness of the intimacy they just shared. She wasn't the first woman to do that to him, but she was the only one that mattered.

"You didn't enjoy it?" she asked, already knowing the answer.

"I more than enjoyed it. I love it and you know it. You know me too well," he said.

Dayton moved away from the dresser and covered Kima's body as he moved them until she was flat on her back. Thankful that she had on a skirt today, he reached underneath of it, removed her panties and before she could say another word, he was inside of her; still hard, still strong and already close to coming again.

"Yes! More, more!" Kima yelled into Dayton's mouth as he kissed her wildly. She wrapped her legs around his waist and took him, not just into her body but even deeper into her heart. "I love you, baby. I love you, I love you, I love you."

Her words drove Dayton on harder and stronger. Kima letting go of her release rocked him into his own second body-stealing orgasm.

Dayton couldn't remember what he was rushing off to do, but whatever it was, it wasn't a priority; only Kima was. He also knew, as his body crested again and again, he was ready for the next level in their lives; he was ready.

15

Hiding out in Australia did not turn out to be an easy task. There were too many people looking for him. Everybody knew his face even after he cut his mustache, dyed his hair black and switched from his usual black pants, white shirt attire to a more casual cream-colored slacks and shirts. Oscar was glad that he had a little hideaway that no one knew about. It wasn't Andrew that he was hiding from, but Carlos. He was the real danger until he could come up with the money he owed him. He did need Andrew's help which is why he grabbed his new cell phone and called him.

"Andy, it's been a minute," he said the minute the man answered.

Being cooped up in a location where he didn't spend much time out and around people had Oscar ready for any contact. His company was being run by its board of directors. Since he'd been missing in action lately, they moved forward without his input. They know they are charged with keeping the raceway going and the circuit in business, despite the fact that their big money draw, Dayton, was no longer racing.

"I could kill you, Oscar. I can't believe you have the nerve to call me after the hundreds of calls and voicemails I've left you have gone unanswered. We haven't heard anything from your daughter and it seems no one has been able to find you since you messed up on taking out that kid. I hear he's alive and well right here in the U.S. I'm going to assume that in place of our deal, you've somehow managed to come up with the thirty million dollars you owe me. I want my money or I want your daughter's company by her marriage to my son. What's it gonna be?" Andrew prodded.

Oscar paced harder than he had been prior to the call. The small cabin he was staying in was a far cry from the six-bedroom, eight-bathroom house he usually occupied in Sydney. He didn't even know if Edna was still at his house. If Kima wasn't going to come to him, he figured out a way to make her go to Sydney. He would make sure she married Nelson even if he had to hogtie her to a chair until the ceremony.

"The marriage is going to happen. I may need another month or two."

"Why should I believe you? You haven't made it happen yet."

Oscar knew he was right but for weeks, he'd been thinking of a master plan. He had to find a reason for Kima to come back to Australia. He couldn't go back to Bozeman to scoop her up. The Sheriff made it clear that if he were to see him again, he would make sure to do a deep dive into Oscar's business. That could spell trouble for him; he didn't want that.

"I have something she wants and I'm going to trick her into coming back here to get it. I'll nab her. She won't defy me anymore. You and Nelson get ready. We can have the ceremony right here in Australia."

"What about the baby? Wasn't it true that she's pregnant by Dayton?" Andrew asked.

The idea of it sickened him while also delighting him. Part of his plan would make him even richer. He'll have Kima and as a result, he knew that Dayton would pay anything to get her back.

"You were right; she is pregnant. I don't know how far. We can twist this to our benefit. She and Nelson can raise this baby as their own, in name only. I don't even know if he really wants her or not, but we don't care, right?" Oscar asked.

He didn't know about Andrew, but he didn't care. The only person he cared about was himself. Perhaps, after the wedding, it was time that Kima found her own life-ending accident. The one reason he never had any kids of his own was because he didn't like them. They were too much of a burden, just as having Kima and her mother around for years had been. Being with them was all about the money and it still was. Kima was in the way.

"I guess he could do that. Nelson will do what I tell him to do. When do you think this will happen?"

Andrew asked and Oscar pondered.

He thought about the most important part of his plan and that was Edna. He needed to find her. Edna is the only person who could get Kima back home. He knew she wouldn't be coming alone. He would deal with Dayton in his own way if he showed up.

"I'm putting my plan in motion this week. Give me a few days and I'll get back to you. Do we still have a deal?"

"Only if I know that you'll deal with that dead weight that's been asking around about you. Who are those guys?"

Oscar didn't want to talk to Andrew about that. That would reveal how he's been stepping on the drugs he's been shipping into Australia and the United States. Andrew would then know that what he was getting wasn't as potent as it was when he bought it from South America. He needed to keep that to himself or Andrew would pull out on their deal.

"I have that covered. That's nothing," he lied.

"Must be something if you're hiding from them. I don't care what else you have going on. Get that girl to the altar and I'll handle my son. Call me when it's done."

"I..."

That was all Oscar got out because the call had ended abruptly. He was tired of Andrew doing that to him. Soon, he'd be free from him too.

"Dammit!" he yelled.

After all the texts and voice messages he'd left Kima over the past few days, it angered him even more that she was showing her lack of respect for him as her father. There had been a time in her life when she worshipped the ground he walked on. She and her mother hung on his every word. He smiled knowing that she would again or she'll be joining her mother. First, he needed to reach out to Edna. Thinking that she may still be at the house, he tried her there first. Before the line rang a second time, he heard her voice – low, but she had answered.

"Edna! Where have you been? Have you been at the house all this time?" he shouted.

"Yes, sir. I didn't have any place else to go."

"Are the men still there?" he asked.

"They come and go, but I don't answer. I stayed inside and didn't go out. Are you coming home, sir?" she asked.

"Uh, no. I'm in Spain with my family. I won't be back for a long while. You can stay at the house. I need you to do something for me," he said.

Oscar could already see his plan in place working out to his benefit.

"Sure, sir. Anything," Edna assured him.

"I know that Kima recently took some boxes from the room upstairs that has all of her mother's old personal things and papers. She's trying to find her father. She's been trying to find him since her mother died."

"Oh, yes, sir. She told me many, many times that she would find him. That's why she took the boxes."

"I figured as much. She left three or four more boxes that will have the information that she needs to find him. I need you to call her and tell her that I told you to go through those things and get rid of them. Tell her if she wants the rest of the boxes, she has to come and get them. She'll ask about me and you have to tell her that I'm in Spain. Tell her that I told you to clean out the house and have it locked up since I'm not coming back."

"Where is she?" Edna asked.

"She's with her boyfriend in America. I don't know which box, but what she needs is in one of the boxes left at the house. You want her to be happy and find her father, right? I know you do because you love Kima like a granddaughter. If you do this to help her, she would be happy forever," Oscar lied. He was using every trick to get Edna onboard without telling her the truth.

"Yes, yes. I don't know if she will come."

"She will if you tell her that I told you to burn the papers and give everything else away. I wish I could do this, but I have business that keeps me away from home. You said you've seen men looking for me? I don't want to see them right now, so I'm stuck here in Spain for a long time. If Kima knows that and she wants the boxes, she'll come home. Can you do this? Can you call her?"

"Yes. I will call her and tell her that you want me to

burn all the boxes and throw all of Ms. Hydea's things in the trash or give them away. If Kima wants any of it, she has to come and get it now because you are in Spain."

"Okay, that's good. Don't tell her I told you to call her. Tell her you are calling on your own because you know she would want her mother's stuff. Understand?"

"I understand."

"Good. Call her tomorrow and tell her I told you to burn them in three days. Say that you don't have a choice because people are coming to lock the house up and change the locks. Do you understand? It has to be three days."

"Three days. Yes, sir. Three days. I will call her tomorrow. Are you closing the house?" she asked him.

"No. I just want Kima to have her stuff. I told you that you can stay in the house. I'll be back in a month. Thanks for your help, Edna. I've always valued you as a member of the family and I know Kima loves you. I'll call back in two days to make sure you called her."

"I will call her tomorrow, surely. She will want all of her mother's things. She misses her; I miss her too. I also miss Kima."

"Well, when she comes home, you will get to see her."

"Thank you for letting me stay in the house. It's really big. I stay downstairs in my quarters and not mess up the rest of the house."

"Good. You know where the money is for your

salary. Only take what I would usually give you each week. That will last until I come back in a month. Thank you, Edna. Thanks for helping me and Kima out."

"Yes, sir."

Oscar threw his phone up in the air and caught it before it hit the floor. His excitement couldn't be contained. Soon, he would have everything he wanted. He could almost smell the victory.

**

"Twins? Who is having twins? Kima? Ah!" Marta screamed. He outburst drew David who raced down the stairs from the second level.

Dayton watched his father head straight for the gun drawer until he saw how happy Marta was and that she wasn't in any danger.

"What the *hell*? I was scared to death. I thought something had happened or someone was in the house," David shouted.

"Oh, David! Dayton just told me the most wonderful news," Marta screamed as she danced around the family room.

"This family and its good news is going to send me to an early grave. Can you not scream like a wild banshee? I thought you were in danger. Let me sit down and calm my racing heart."

David placed his hand over his chest. Dayton laughed knowing his father was exaggerating as only he could.

"Pop, you good?" Dayton asked, buying into the drama.

"I will be when I hear this news. What is it?"

"Kima and I found out that she's having two babies, not one. She's carrying twins, Pop. Can you believe that?"

David quickly stood back up.

"Two? That's wonderful news. Now I know why your mother is dancing around like this."

David danced with her when she pulled him into an embrace.

"When did you find out, son?" David asked.

"Just this morning. She had her first appointment for a sonogram with the doctor who'll, hopefully, be delivering the baby. Kima was concerned about her weight gain. She was already carrying pretty big for someone three-months along."

"Could you tell what they were?" Marta asked.

"No, Ma. Not yet. We want to know, so the moment the doctor can tell us, we'll let you know."

"Where's Kima?"

"After that news, she wanted to go lay down. She was prepared for one, but two? She's nervous and scared."

"Nonsense. She has all of us. I've been meaning to ask you about any luck finding her father; not Oscar, but her father."

Dayton exhaled through his frustration.

"We hired some people to help her look, but so far,

nothing. We've been over the papers she brought with her from home, but what she has isn't enough. She's mad that she left so much there."

"Keep trying. I know something will come of it. Nothing from Oscar?" Marta queried.

Everyone in the family was surprised that Oscar hadn't made any attempts to come back to the ranch. They had no idea where he was. He'd sent quite a few texts to Kima, still making demands up to a few days ago. She'd also told him that Oscar had also left voice mail messages screaming and making further demands that way as well. Dayton was happy when she said when she heard his tone on each one, she deleted it before listening to it. They were happy and she wouldn't let Oscar's madness mess anything up.

"Kima thinks he's in Spain, hiding out from some people. She's checked in with some friends who told her that there are people trying really hard to find him. None of them have seen him and you can't really miss him when you see him."

"Well, at least he's not here. Did you see that Nick and Parker are back from their month-long trip? Can you believe they were gone that long?" Marta asked.

"Yeah, he called me this morning to say they had landed. He wanted to know how Kima was doing. I'm going to head over there after I raid your fridge for some fresh fruit for Kima. She's madly in love with the grapes and watermelon. Do you have any cut up already or can I cut some for her?" Dayton asked.

"There is plenty already cut; I think there are three big bowls. Take as much as you want and take all the grapes in there. I'll make sure there is more later today."

"You're the best. Kima didn't believe me when I told her that we grow our own fruit right here on the ranch. She can't stop eating it."

"I'll send extra over so that she doesn't run out. She's eating for three now. Imagine that!" Marta called out.

Dayton couldn't believe it either. He was more excited than ever as he raced off to the kitchen. He was grateful for the reprieve and needed to be alone. He, like Kima, was nervous about the idea of having two babies at the same time. He almost fainted himself when the doctor came in saying the results showed two babies. He was having two of them at one time. Now, more than ever, it was time to have that permanent connection with Kima. The ring he'd been holding on to was about to find its place on her hand.

Grabbing what he needed, Dayton walked back through the house, finding it empty. Once he jumped in his truck and turned to head back to his house, Kima was calling him.

"Hey, baby! I'm on my way."

When she should have responded, he didn't hear anything. Listening closer, he thought he heard silent sobs.

"Day, how far away are you?" she finally said.

"What's wrong?"

He didn't wait for an answer before smashing the pedal to the floor of the truck and it took off. Being a racecar driver had its benefits.

"I got a call just now from Edna. She said my father left for Spain and told her to burn the papers that were left in the attic. She is then to get rid of all of my mother's things. He's closing up the house and not coming back for a while. Can you believe how cruel he is being? He wants to destroy everything I have left that belongs to my mother. What if what I need to find my father is in those boxes?"

When Kima started to bawl, Dayton had just reached the front of his house. Barely turning his truck off, he raced inside and found Kima sitting on the sofa in the great room. He immediately took her into his arms after sliding onto the sofa and pulling her onto his lap.

"You scared me. I thought something was wrong with you or the baby," he said, trying to calm his beating heart.

"Something is wrong! I need my mother's things. Can we please go to get them? He's not in Australia and you'll be with me. Edna said he told her to have the house closed up and the locks changed in three days."

Dayton wiped the tears that streamed down her face. He once told her that he wouldn't deny her anything and he meant that.

"Baby, we'll leave first thing in the morning. Let me

call Shelton to see if he can get us arrangements. We'll get your things and come right back. You said Edna said he called her from Spain? Then we can be in and out of there in no time at all. We won't let him wipe out all traces of your mother as if she didn't exist. I got you, Kima. You know I got you, baby."

Dayton let her cry it out. Five minutes later, she had cried herself to sleep. Sliding her from his lap to the soft sofa, he covered her with a blanket that was nearby. He needed to talk to Shelton now; his thought as he moved to the kitchen to make the call.

Shelton had been spending a lot of time at the Sheriff's office and wondered if he was there, at home or on the ranch. Wherever he was, Dayton needed him to drop everything and get him and Kima back to Australia with a quickness.

16

Oscar stretched his neck as far as he could as he tried to find any sign of Andrew and Nelson whose plane should have arrived an hour ago. He was late meeting them because he wanted to check to be sure Kima hadn't left Sydney yet.

With his dark sunglasses, he couldn't see much. He pulled his brown Fedora down over his face as much as he could. Out of the corner of his eye, he saw Nelson first, who was much taller than his father. He waved them over as he found a hidden spot behind a tall potted plan.

"What the hell are you doing hiding? You must have really pissed off some bad people," Andrew claimed.

"Yeah, whatever. Are you ready? I don't know how much of a window we're going to have. They've been here a day. I had some people check and they are scheduled to fly out tomorrow night. This has to happen now. Kima is at her place."

"Is she alone?" Andrew asked.

"Dad, this is a bad idea. You can't make her marry me like this. This whole thing is a catastrophe."

Oscar watched Andrew pull Nelson along with a tight death grip on his arm. No one said anything else until they were seated in the back of the long black limousine Oscar had secured. He'd already had Andrew's favorite bottles chilling on ice, hoping to make up for the mess he's caused with the delay in Kima and Nelson getting married.

"Nelson, before you say another word, you listen to me clearly."

Oscar leaned back in his chair after giving the driver the address to Kima's flat where he'd already had a few of his guys keeping watch that she was still alone. As he suspected, Dayton couldn't pass up the opportunity to get behind a car at the track. There wasn't a track in Montana even close to what Australia had. He knew it would be a sure thing to have a friend of Dayton's from his team run into him and share about a new car on the track that he bet Dayton would want to check out. When the report came back about the excitement in Dayton's eyes, he knew there was no way Kima would be against him getting in one last ride.

"Dad, you know this is crazy! You are talking about kidnapping a woman and threatening her life and that of her unborn child and boyfriend unless she marries me. You think I want a woman like that?" Nelson whined.

Oscar could see Andrew's patience waning.

"You will marry whoever I tell you to marry and you'll like it even if you don't. I don't care if it's a wedding in name only. You can screw a hundred women behind her back or even in her face. I need you married so that you can claim her company and we can combine it with ours. It's not hard. You can call this whatever you want, I don't care. He's her father and he's putting this all in place. Her own father, boy! You will marry her and you'll do it today. Did you take care of everything?" Andrew asked Oscar.

"If you mean securing the paperwork for this quickie wedding? I sure did. This is actually easier than I thought it was going to be. I have always believed that people with money can buy anything and anyone; both worked in this instance. This paperwork cost me a small fortune," he admitted.

"Whatever it takes, right?" Andrew cheered, pouring himself a drink.

"I assumed I'd have to come up with something to do with Dayton, but he took care of that for me himself out of his love for fast cars. He'll be a minute, which is why we are heading straight for her flat. She's already taken what she wanted from the house, thanks to Edna. She and that boy were together the whole time, so snatching her there was complicated. Plus, Edna was there."

"I can't believe you're making me do this. There has to be a better way. What about what I want for my life? I don't even know Kima. Who marries a woman they don't know?"

"You do and you will or you'll end up with nothing. How do you think you'll fair without the Gaynor money? Do this or you won't have even a penny to your name. Gone will be your cars, your house, your condo and all those expensive trips and parties. Think long and hard. I don't ask you for much. I don't care if you drop her like a hot potato in a year – for right now, you will do this. As long as you stay her husband for a year and a day, according to Oscar here, what is hers will be yours. You will convince her that you know what's best for her interest and sign everything over to me. I'll take it from there. Oscar here will get his money, I'll double my wealth for now and in the future and you'll have a pretty little thing to do whatever you want," Andrew explained.

"Dad! She's pregnant! You told me she's pregnant! This is insane! Let me out of this car. I never should have gotten on that plane," Nelson yelled and reached for the door handle, which did not open.

Andrew quickly snatched him up by his designer shirt. Knowing his son's flair for all things designer and high-end, he had no doubt Nelson would end up doing what he asked.

"The future of my company is at stake. I have people counting on this merger and you will follow through and help me on this. We're talking being married for one year; just one year. You can walk away after that."

"She's pregnant by a man she loves. You think she's going to give that up because you tell her to? That's not right. What if someone did that to Rachel? What would you do? Would you make your own daughter, my baby sister, do something like this for money? There are better ways to do business."

Nelson was pleading for his life. He hadn't said much before now because he assumed Kima would never go through with this fake marriage all because her father wanted to play a dangerous game of let's make a deal. His latest mistake was getting on the plane with his father when Oscar called the day before saying his daughter was back home. He told them to get to Sydney right away. Before the sun came up on another day, there would be a marriage. Knowing anything else he said would fall on his father's deaf ears, Nelson slumped back in his seat and waited. He had to figure out a way out of this. He had done a lot of things for his father, some legal and some illegal, but marrying a woman who doesn't want to marry him and he doesn't want to marry, that's going too far. He never thought he would see the day that his father would stoop so low. In his eyes, Andrew Gaynor had reached rock bottom. He couldn't go any lower.

"I would never let anyone even touch my daughter let alone make her marry anyone, but I'm not Oscar, am I?" Andrew explained.

Oscar started to defend himself, but he was already admitting to himself that he was a deviant. All he had to say for himself was that he had a plan for his life and it was to get and stay rich. If Kima's happiness had to be the casualty, so be it. If she was stupid enough to return to the scene of the crime along with her boyfriend, she deserved what was coming to her and so did he.

Nelson turned toward the window, away from his father and Oscar who were already celebrating with liquor. He found nothing to celebrate about. He also knew that he was ready to give up everything monetary that his father held in such high esteem. He already had a woman in his own life that he was planning to marry. They have plans for a nice, small wedding in Las Vegas with only his sister and his mother from his family in attendance. His father would seek vengeance but he didn't care. At thirty-one, it was time he lived his own life. How he was going to get to that, he didn't know. Soon they would have Kima in their clutches and all would be lost; or perhaps not.

With his body turned away from them as they drank and toasted to everything under the sun, Nelson slipped his cell phone out of his suit jacket pocket and found the number that had been texted to him while he was on the plane. His father didn't know it but the planning that was done was about to be interrupted.

Nelson had reached out to a few racecar driving friends and got what he needed. If he was going to stop this wedding, he needed help. There was only one person he knew of who had as much stake in this fake marriage not taking place as he did; that person was Dayton Sullivan. He only hoped it wasn't too late to finally take action, something he should have done months ago when his father first approached his with his outlandish scheme.

Pretending to be taking in the sites, Nelson typed out a text and hoped to hell that Dayton got it in time. Everything counted on Dayton's love and devotion to Kima.

17

Dayton brought the Chevrolet Camaro ZL1 to a complete stop after three times around the track, familiarizing himself with his love for speed. He didn't realize how much he'd missed the track until he got behind the wheel of Zach's car.

He hadn't seen Zach since he was last in Sydney for the race he didn't get to take part in. Zach had won that day. Trying to pump up Dayton's ego, his friend actually thanked him for not racing. Zach was finally happy to get himself in the winner's circle. Dayton didn't know how to take that comment, but he let it go. He was too excited about the car. Either way, he was glad that he happened to run into Zach as he and Kima were getting out of their rental car at her flat. Zach mentioned that he happened to be there visiting a female friend. They talked a little and when Zach told him that he should take one last ride on the Sydney raceway, he found it hard to pass up on the chance to do so. Knowing he wouldn't run into Oscar, though he knew others would eventually tell him that they saw him, he didn't care. The draw to test out Zach's new car was strong.

Once Kima said she would be fine grabbing what she needed and would pick him up at the track within an hour, he took Zach up on the offer. It wasn't until he was about to do a fourth lap that he realized he hadn't heard from Kima. As he drove around, he didn't see her pull up to the track. His mind went back to the night in the hotel when he and Kima first arrived on Bozeman. He'd had a terrible nightmare. The scene was right here at this track. That made him not want to do another lap around. He wondered what was keeping her.

"What? I thought you would have done at least three or four more laps around. Isn't she fast? She's the fastest I've ever had. Man, I was watching you grip those curves as only the great Dayton Sullivan could drive. When Mr. Oscar suggested..."

Every part of Dayton froze. The minute he looked at Zach, he knew this wasn't good. His heart began to beat as loud as a drum in his chest. He could hear it in his ears. He looked around at the empty track, but still, his nightmare surface. Things didn't look the same, but they still felt the same. Zach had caught himself, but not before Dayton heard every word.

"What did you say about Oscar?" he yelled with forceful anger.

Unzipping his racing gear with the speed of lightning, Dayton grabbed Zach by the collar and dragged him back against the large silver fence.

"What? What are you doing? Let me go. What did

I do?" Zach pleaded.

"It wasn't about what you did or it could be. It's about what you said or maybe didn't say, yet. You said Oscar suggested. What did he suggest? What were you going to say?"

Dayton saw the terror in Zach's eyes because the rage in his own could be seen miles away. Any minute, Zach was about to suffer many painful blows if he didn't spill. He thought back to Perry's story about how he was willing to beat the life out of Gizelle's ex-husband when he realized that the man intended to kill her. His rage got the best of him just as Dayton's was controlling him. Zach took a big gulp before he spoke.

"Man, I swear, I wasn't going to say anything. I simply misspoke."

Dayton heard the words but didn't believe it. Oscar was somehow involved, but how? The man was in Spain. What could he do from there? Zach was going to tell him or he was about to wish he had.

Dayton picked him up effortlessly and slammed him back against the fence with all of this might. When Zach doubled over in pain, he held him tight, prepared to repeat the move until he winced louder.

"What were you going to say? Now Zach!" Dayton shouted.

When he reared his arm back and balled up his fist, Zach gave up.

"Alright, alright. Just don't hit me. I bruise easily. It wasn't a coincidence that we ran into each other today outside of Kima's building. Mr. Oscar had me staking out her spot since yesterday. He said when you and Kima arrived, if you did, that I was to act like I was visiting someone. I was then instructed to text him that you had arrived. He already knew you were here."

Dayton reached for his phone while Zach talked. He dialed Kima again and again and got no answer. His heart was racing fiercely as sheer terror took over.

"I'm here now because he set this up? Is he in Sydney? Is Oscar here?" Dayton yelled, pulling his grip tighter.

"Man, I don't know. Just let me go. He gave me five thousand dollars to get you here. That's all I know."

"Last time, Zach. Is Oscar in Sydney!"

"Yes. He was at Kima's flat this morning when he gave me the money. He's got some guys there who were waiting for her."

"Oh my god! I left her *alone*! I left Kima alone and I knew I shouldn't have. Something told me not to."

"Maybe you shouldn't have," Zach said. Any other words he was about to speak were cut off with a hard punch to his gut.

"That's for setting me and my girl up."

"Ugh," Zach screamed in pain.

Dayton hit him again.

"That's for taking part in Oscar's scheme. He wants to hurt her you clown! Your car? Where are your keys? Give me the keys!"

When Zach raised the keys up as he doubled over

from the pain, without hesitating, Dayton snatched the keys to the car Zach had driven them to the raceway in. He didn't jog, he sprinted as fast as he could. Unlike his dream, he was actually moving fast knowing now that Kima was really in danger. Barely waiting for the door to close, he had the car in drive in less than a second, if that was possible. He hit the streets of Sydney as if he were still on the race track. His babies, Kima and their babies, were in danger. If anything happened to them, he wouldn't forgive himself.

Grabbing his phone as he whizzed in and out of traffic, he called the only true friend he had in Australia. When he told Rusty he was flying in for two days, Rusty wanted to talk to him and flew in from Europe where he was visiting his wife's family.

Before he could say Rusty's name for the speed dial, his phone pinged. Hoping it was Kima, he checked it. It was from a number he didn't recognize. As he read the message, he saw that he nearly hit a car when he sped through a red light. There would be no slowing down. The message only made him speed up faster. It read:

"Dayton, this is not a joke. This is the man that Oscar is trying to marry Kima off to today. He knows you're in Sydney and Kima is in danger. If you are not with her, you need to get to her. We are heading to her flat right now. We'll be there in ten minutes. Oscar plans to kidnap her. Get to her and do it now. I will help when I can. Nelson."

That was it. Dayton was mad enough to kill someone. He then dialed Rusty.

"Rusty, before you speak, listen to me. Where are you?"

"I'm about a minute from that restaurant we agreed to meet at two blocks from Kima's place. Where are you?" he asked.

"Oscar is in Sydney. He's not in Spain. That was all a lie. It was a plan to get Kima back here. Our being here was some kind of trap. I was stupid enough to allow myself to be lured away to the track, leaving her alone. I never should have done that. There are people who plan to kidnap her. It's happening right now. Can you meet me there?"

"You damn right I can. I have one of my guys with me too. He wanted to chat with you about racing and was going to join us for dinner. How far away are you?"

"I'm pulling up right now. I scared myself with how fast I got here. I pulled in a space out of view of Kima's windows. There is a limo parked in front of the building. Something tells me that's Oscar."

"I'm here, kid. I'm going to pull around to the back and come at it that way."

"Those doors are locked."

"Dayton, never underestimate me. I wasn't always just a business manager. I've broken a law or two in my day and in that day, a lot of what I did that was illegal involved getting into doors people thought they could keep me out of. Pull around here and meet me right now. Don't worry, we got this. If they're still here, they'll wish they weren't. Oscar is a punk. He doesn't want this smoke."

Dayton did just that. The minute he saw Rusty and the guy who was with him, no words were needed. They raced to the door and within sixty seconds, Rusty had the door opened. They made their way up the stairwell, moving like ninjas. Adrenaline was pumping. All Dayton wanted to do was get his hands on Oscar. He only a few minutes alone with him. Boxing and karate lessons he took as a kid would be put to great use. As they made their way up, Dayton prayed that Kima and his babies were okay; they had to be.

18

Kima was excited when she heard the knock on the door. Thinking it was Dayton coming back before she could get to him, she pulled the door open without checking to see who was on the other side. She was shocked to see her father, Andrew and Nelson.

"You couldn't resist coming back after Edna called you, huh? That, my dear daughter, was all me," Oscar gloated and leered in her face.

Kima backed up in fear just as Oscar grabbed her wrist and held her in place. She tried to struggle, but that only made his grip grow tighter, hurting her.

"Let go of me!" she screamed.

Oscar jerked her toward his face.

"Do that again and I'll tape up your mouth. You're leaving here with me right now. We have an appointment with a priest who is going to marry you and Nelson. I'm tired of waiting on you to come around."

"I'll scream when I get there and tell the priest what you are doing!" she yelled, rebelliously.

"Haven't you learned anything about me after all of

these years? Money buys everyone, including a priest," Oscar mocked.

Kima reached for her stomach as Oscars eyes followed where her hand rested.

"She sure is pregnant," Andrew exclaimed. "Come on Oscar, we have to leave. People will come out if they hear this ruckus," he added.

"There won't be any noise, will there, Kima? Because see, she wouldn't want anything to happen to her baby or to Dayton. I bet you're wondering where he is." Oscar leaned close to her ear. "I know where he is. I'm still debating on whether he'll get to live or not. Cooperate and you may not be able to marry him, but at least you'll know he won't be dead. Now, walk and don't you try and scream or do anything crazy. I would hate for you to miss a step and fall flat on your stomach. That would be a shame."

"You're an awful man," Nelson said. "You and my father are both mad," he growled out.

"Shut up, Nelson and watch the door," Andrew demanded.

Standing in the doorway, Nelson saw movement out of the corner of his eye. Lowering his hand behind his back, he signaled for Dayton and the two men with him to come forward. He was happy that Dayton got his message.

Dayton was about to storm the door when Rusty pulls him back. He watched him mouth to Nelson to play along and Nelson nodded that he understood.

Without warning, Rusty reached the door, grabbed Nelson, putting him in a choke hold with a knife up to his neck. Everyone in the room turned at the sound. Before anything could think of how to respond, Dayton did move. He couldn't wait a second longer when he saw Kima being manhandled by her father. He raced for Oscar. Dayton didn't wait for anyone to tell him what to do. He didn't care that Oscar was Kima's father. He placed both of his hands around the fat man's neck and squeezed. Out of the corner of his eye, he saw Andrew trying to make run for the door. The man that had come with him and Rusty clipped him just as he raced across the floor, falling face-first. Dayton turned his attention back to the man at hand.

Placing his face right up against Oscars, Dayton spoke directly to the man, making sure there was no doubt that if he didn't listen, things were not going to end well for him.

"Get your hand off of her or her wrist will be the last thing you will feel on this side of life," he warned.

Before Oscar could throw his weight around as he usually did, they all heard the sound of sirens approaching the building.

"Yeah, they are for you, old man," Rusty said as he let go of Nelson. "Sorry for that, son, but I needed to get into the room and surprise them with the possibility of you getting harmed," Rusty explained.

"Let her go, Oscar. This is your last warning. Ask Zach how serious I am when it comes to Kima. He's probably still kissing the asphalt where I left him after he let it slip that you were here."

Between the sirens, Rusty with a long, sharp blade now at Oscar's neck next to where Dayton's hands were, Oscar released Kima and Dayton pulled her into his arms. He moved away from Oscar with her as the man sounded like he was hacking up a long in the struggle to breathe. Dayton knew how tight his hands had been around his neck and didn't care. He let Rusty take over. He needed to get Kima away from the sight before her.

"You're okay? You're okay!" Kima shouted and peppered Dayton's face with so many kisses that there couldn't be a place on his face that her lips hadn't just touch.

"Yes, I'm fine. Are you okay?" he asked, checking her out as much as he could.

"Yes, I'm okay. He's a lunatic. He was going to drag me out to some priest to marry me off to Nelson tonight."

"I don't think that was going to happen. Even though Zach let it slip that running into us here was not a coincidence, but a staged meeting set up by Oscar, Nelson sent me a text telling me that you were in danger and that I needed to get here right away. I called Rusty who was already planning to meet us for dinner. I'm so sorry I left you alone. That will never happen again. The thought that I could have lost you and our babies was a fear I never want to experience again."

Pulling Kima close, Dayton moved when the elevator doors opened and out poured four members of the Australian Federal Police.

"They're in here," Rusty pointed before joining Kima and Dayton. "Are you okay, little one?" Rusty asked Kima.

Kima smiled and nodded. She loved that Rusty has always called her that.

"I am."

"How did the cops find out about this?" Dayton asked.

"I called them right when I arrived. I told them that the owner of TOBIT Motorsports Raceway was about to be kidnapped."

"Good looking out," Dayton said. He didn't wait around for what was going to happen to Oscar. He took Kima and walked into the elevator. Once outside, they walked with her head on his shoulder.

"I know you're going to squawk about this, but you need a hospital to check you over. Don't tell me you're fine. I need a doctor to confirm that while I call my family. You're okay, baby. That's all that matters."

"You're okay too and that's all that matters to me; well, you and our babies," Kima said.

Before getting in the car after Dayton opened the door, Kima turned and faced him.

"What?" he asked.

"I want to leave here and never come back. I don't know what to do about the company or anything else here, but I want it all in my rearview mirror. I want our life in Montana. I may never find my real father, but the love of your family is what I have longed for since my mother died. You are enough for me. They are enough for me. I just want us," she pleaded. "What Oscar tried to do to me was the last straw. His action just now was my sign that he is dead to me."

"He'll be in jail before we get to the airport. He tried to kidnap you. He assaulted you when he grabbed your wrist like that. He's a menace. Getting him out of our live is the best suggestion you've made since I've met you."

When Dayton smiled at her with every tooth in his mouth, Kima didn't know what was running through his head.

"I'm thinking that before we are mommy and daddy, we need to be husband and wife. I want you to be my wife. Now, this isn't my official proposal or anything. I mean, I do have a ring and everything back at home. I want to do it right. I just want you to know that I want to do it before the babies are born."

"I can't wait. At least our wedding won't be a shotgun wedding. Do you think the police will need to talk to me?" she asked.

"I'm sure they will, but right now, get in the car and let's get you checked out. We'll talk to them after. First, I need to call my brothers and convince them to not jump on a plane and threaten everyone in Sydney."

"I love your family," Kima said as she waited for

Dayton to get in on the other side. When he leaned in her direction and captured her lips, they didn't need words. They only needed to taste and feel.

Dayton pulled away but spoke pointedly with no hesitation in his voice.

"They are your family, too."

Dayton started up the car, a Toyota Camry and Kima looked around.

"You're literally going to drive Zach's car like it's nothing?" she asked.

"I sure am. He's lucky I left him with his teeth and no broken bones. I'll leave it someplace and he can figure out how to find it. We're going to wrap up our visit tomorrow, take everything you need and make our way home."

"What about Zach? He was a part of this too?" she asked.

"Like so many others, he was a pawn in this. He didn't know what he was doing. He's young. I don't want to ruin his chance to do things right going forward. I just want to take you and our family home."

"Home," Kima said. She loved the sound of that.

**

"Where is she, Day? You're sure she's okay?" Nick said on speaker phone with the rest of this family in the background.

When he called Nick, he had no idea his brother would rush to the main house after calling everyone and getting them in one place. He and Kima had left the hospital where they were told she was fine. Her arm would be bruised where Oscar held it tight, but she would be fine. After an hour of being questioned by the police, they were finally able to leave the police station to go back to Kima's place. They didn't stay long after Rusty agreed to have her entire flat packed up and everything shipped to Montana. The boxes Kima took from her father's house along with bags of her mother's belongings that she wanted to keep, they were taking with them on the plane in the morning. Kima refused to let those items out of her sight.

"She's asleep. After the doctor checked her out, I got us a room and before I could run her a bath, she was already asleep."

"You should be asleep too," Marta yelled out. "Why didn't you get back on the jet?" she asked.

"I needed to slow things down for her. It's been a wild ride," he explained.

"It's a good thing you cleared that up because I was about to have the Sully II ready to take me and Shelton to Australia," Perry said.

Dayton didn't doubt it. Shelton had sent him and Kima on the other jet, Sully I, which was gassed up and ready to fly back to the states. Kima wanted to shower and lay in a bed. Just to be safe, Rusty had guys watching their room until they were ready to leave.

"Yeah, and be prepared for me and Shelton to be at the airport when you land. You already know why," Perry said and everyone in the room with them laughed.

Dayton chuckled too.

"Yeah, I know. Mom threatened your life if you didn't get here to pick up me and Kima so that we don't make any more stops before the ranch," Dayton declared.

"Actually, she threatened us about making sure her grandbabies got back to the ranch safe. You do know that you and Kima are literally chopped liver now. It's all about the babies. We're glad you're both okay. What happened sounded pretty scary," David said.

"It was, Pop. You know Rusty saved the day," Dayton admitted.

"Make sure you tell him we are indebted to him," Marta said.

"You can tell him. He'll be in Montana in about a week. He said it's been a while since his wife and kids have been to the ranch. He claims they are in dire need of a vacation."

"Oh, that's wonderful. I'll have Brielle set them up in a large cabin and sign the kids up for some fun activities. We can't wait to see him," Marta explained.

"Alright, y'all. My body is coming down from the rush of all that happened. I want to go kiss and love on my woman. We'll see you tomorrow. Ma, start preparing for another wedding. It needs to take place before the babies are born," Dayton said to loud cheers from the other end of the phone.

"I'm all over that!" Brielle yelled.

Dayton heard Shelton take the phone off of speaker.

"Day, listen, there is one more thing that I want to talk to you about. I don't want to do it when you arrive in the morning and Kima is with you at the airport."

"What is it?"

"I think my people may have found Kima's father. Remember the files that were sent from that lawyer's wife? The one who died in the boating accident?"

"Yeah. What about them?"

Dayton could feel his excitement rising. Were they actually going to be able to find Kima's father?

"McKenna and I have been going over them with my people and they found a folder with a computer jump drive in it. On it are several pictures of Kima's mother when she was pregnant and she's with a man. McKenna was able to use her connections at Homeland Security to get us access to facial recognition software. I think we found him. Do you want to tell Kima tomorrow?" Shelton asked.

Dayton looked toward the bed. Kima has had enough excitement, good and bad. In case this didn't pan out, he didn't want her hyped up only to snatch the rug from under her. He needed to know for sure before telling her.

"No. Not just yet. Let's talk about it when I get home. Wait, did you say McKenna? She's McKenna now and not Deputy Sheriff McKenna Gibson?" Dayton asked.

The few times Dayton had seen her and Shelton in the same room, he sensed something was up between them. She started out doing a favor for Marcus in helping them with following leads on Kima's father. In the last week before he and Kima headed back to Australia, McKenna could be seen on the ranch when she wasn't on the clock. He knew his brother loved beautiful women and that was definitely McKenna, especially out of uniform.

"Don't go there, Day. It's all business. You'll want to thank her. Her connections got us this far."

"I'll thank her when we get back. You sure you don't want to do your own brand of thanking her for me?" he asked all snarky-like.

Dayton waited for Shelton's retort and was shocked he didn't get one. He knew at that moment that he'd hit a nerve.

"See you in the morning, Day. Take care of Kima."

"Done," Dayton said to himself since Shelton had already hung up.

Turning out the lights and casting the bedroom of their hotel suite into total darkness he walked over to the bed and slid in close to Kima's body.

"Day?" Kima said pulling his arms tighter around her body from where he snuggled up close behind her.

"I'm here baby. I'm never going anywhere again."

"It's okay if you do. I know that you'll come back to me. There have been so many times between my father's drama and the risks of racecar driving that I could have lost you. I don't want to live thinking we can't be out of each other's sight. I told you, I just want us. I love you so much. You're giving me something I haven't had since my mother; you're giving me a family. I feel so loved by all of you. I can't ask for more than that."

Dayton kissed her bare shoulder and placed his hand on her belly and held it there. He wanted to give her more hope that she may have more family out in the world, but he would wait.

"I love you, too. My brothers will be at the airport when we land in the morning. Everyone is on pins and needles until you're back home. Be prepared to be pampered. They were scared when I first told them what happened. We'll be home before we know it. Go back to sleep, baby."

"I want love," Kima slurred.

Dayton snickered. After the crazy day they just had, she wanted sex. Rather than address it, he let the silence woo her back to sleep. He didn't think he would have the strength. That story would change as soon as they were back home and in their own bed. He would love her as often as she needed and wanted. Nothing was over their heads anymore. They were finally free to just love.

19

Five months later – Sullivan Ranch

Dayton walked up the stairs in his parents' home to find Kima still fussing with her hair. She was a beautiful vision before him sitting at the small marble white and gold table and chair with a large lighted mirror on it. He remembered his sister calling this a make-up table years ago when she'd gotten one like it for her bedroom.

Parker, Gizelle and Brielle moved about fussing over every aspect of Kima's appearance from her hair, makeup, jewelry and her dress. They smiled, like only women who understand what the day means could do. Everyone on the ranch fell in line to making this exactly what Kima would for, what is, her wedding day. Dayton was happy that him being in the room, gazing upon his bride wasn't a surprise to anyone. Most women, especially the bride, would go ballistic if the groom saw her on her wedding day before the ceremony. Kima made it known early that she didn't believe in superstitions and old traditions. She wanted things her way and so did he. Considering she was going to give birth to twin boys sooner than they all thought, according to her doctor, she wanted her entire day to be about her and Dayton. They were assured that giving a few weeks shy of her delivery date was okay. He trusted the medical professionals who convinced him the babies and Kima would be fine.

For the wedding, they also decided to go with a less formal one than what Perry and Nick had done as far as attire. Dayton looked down and checked himself out. He was donned in a dark blue casual suit, crisp white shirt and white and blue Nike Court Air Zoom Vapor Cage 4 sneakers. His only jewelry, for now, was the new platinum Santos De Cartier watch that was gifted to him the night before from his wife-to-be.

Looking around the room that at one time had been Brielle's bedroom, now transformed into a walk-in dressing room for his mother, Dayton leaned against the door and watched everyone work. The moment Kima caught a glimpse of him in the mirror, the smile she sported lit up, not only the room, but Dayton's entire life. This was happening for them today. They were about to become husband and wife within the hour.

"You like?" Kima asked, leaning on Brielle for support in order to turn around in the seat. Two babies at a little over eight months was no easy task even for the everyday activity of turning around.

"I love," he replied. When he blew a kiss her way, Kima, not being bashful that family was in the room, caught that kiss and placed it right in the center of one of her breasts.

"Stop that kinky stuff! I've learned what that means between the two of you. None of that. We have a wedding to get to. I told you and Dayton to keep it in his pants and under your dress until later tonight," Brielle warned playfully.

"So bossy!" Dayton hollered.

"My nephews aren't going to know what the world is like, coming out thinking every moment is an earthquake with all that loving the two of you do. Don't start nothing!" Brielle yelled. The room broke out in laughter by everyone except Dayton. He did not enjoy having his personal life as the fodder for everyone.

"Really? Should I speak loud about the guy I see creeping from your house at the wee hours of the morning? Oh, wait? He's a bunkhouse guy, right?" Dayton exclaimed.

When Brielle's mouth formed a large circle as she looked from Gizelle to Parker then to Kima, he knew she wanted to kill him.

"Day!" Kima said defensively.

"You're doing a bunkhouse guy?" Parker yelled and then covered her mouth when Brielle punched her good-humoredly on the shoulder.

"What? Like I didn't catch you and Nick up in the barn with your legs high in the air? I bet you're still picking out hay from all of your nook and crannies," Brielle retorted.

"You saw that?" Parker yelled.

"Damn right I did."

Dayton held a steady face as Kima tried her best to hold in her belly-rolling, full-blown laugh fest.

"Both of you need to stop. This is about Kima and Dayton's wedding day. Not your wild sex lives," Gizelle joined in with her motherly advice. One month after delivering her own baby girl, she looked amazing in her royal blue, tea length dress, barely any signs that she'd just had a baby.

Dayton knew it was on when Parker stopped laughing, put both of her hands on her hips and swung her head around in Gizelle's direction as wide as she could.

"I know you're not talking about our wild sex lives. How about, I was babysitting Carrie and Brody until eight one night a few months back. I was taking them home, walked up the steps to their brand-new house and opened the door. It's a good thing the kids were playing in the grass and didn't follow me right up. What did my eyes see before I wanted to scratch them out? I saw Gizelle riding Perry like he was a stallion while he howled at the moon."

Gizelle pouted while everyone laughed. Dayton didn't dare join in. He knew better. If he did, all the women would turn on him and he didn't have any of his brothers to have his back.

"I forgot you were bringing them home at eight. Perry had just gotten in, we were alone and the moment took over. He can't howl like that with the kids home!" Gizelle protested and then laughed at herself.

"Well next time, lock the damn door!" Parker hollered.

"Y'all are all crazy! I should not be hearing this!" Dayton exclaimed and moved into the room to stand in front of Kima.

"I said no kinky stuff. We're still in the room here," Brielle yelled.

"Alright, now that we've all had our sex lives aired out on this day, Kima, I think you're ready," Parker said.

"Can you give us a minute?" Dayton asked, his eyes focused on Kima.

When he looked between each of the other woman in the room, they nodded since they knew why he needed to clear the room. Kima was the only person who was about to be either surprised or shocked.

When they left and closed the door, he helped Kima stand to her feet. Spinning her around slowly, he took in her long, cream, silk Vera Wang chiffon maternity evening gown which included a pleated cinched bust and gold off-the-shoulder straps. He knew those specifics because Kima had been speaking of it since the moment she and Brielle had picked out the dress together. This was his first time seeing her in it. When he looked down to her feet, he hadn't been expecting to see any type of high-heeled shoe, but she surprised him with her high-top Air Force One sneakers. They really did go the non-traditional route.

Kima's hair was pulled up into a tight bun and as usual, her makeup was minimal, but flawless. Her natural beauty was all she needed. That was a sentiment he bestowed on her daily. I loved everything about her just the way she was. The only time she needed to make a change was if she wanted to do so for herself.

Around her neck was his gift to her the night before. It was a Monica Rich Kosann™ Four Image Premier Diamond Locket. The four image holders will soon hold pictures of them along with their boys, Austin and Dustin, arriving in a week via a C-section. Yes, the world could definitely use more Sullivans. The moment he placed the charm around her neck, Kima vowed that she would never, ever take it off.

"Well?" she asked after finally turning back around to face him.

"You are glowing," Dayton said placing his hands on her stomach. "I'm ready for your name to change to Sullivan, I know that. What about you?" he asked.

"I was ready a long time ago. Today will be perfect. I don't think it could get any better than this; me and you walking down the aisle together in front of all of our friends and your family. I was so happy that Nala and Bridget made it in town a few days ago. Thanks for putting them up in their own cabins. It was good to hang out with them for a full night the day they arrived. I know you missed me in bed with you."

"I did, but I know what it meant for you to have them here."

"Now, you know they may never leave. They got their looks at all of those bunkhouse boys. Nala has already extended her stay by a week. Bridget is still trying to get extra days off from work so that she can stay longer too."

"Baby, your friends can stay as long as they like."

"What about Edna? Can you believe she actually came? I know she felt bad that my father lured her into his web of lies."

Dayton nodded, happy that things worked out.

"She couldn't have known what he was trying to do. I'm just glad that she has decided to stay here on the ranch with us for good to help you with the babies. We're still working on her visa and going through the process for her to become an American citizen."

"I have never seen her happier. Today is perfect, right?" Kima exclaimed.

Dayton knew that now was the best time to get his news out. He was inwardly hoping and praying that what he'd done was a good thing.

"Baby, why don't you sit down. I have something I want to talk to you about."

Worried, Kima sat but kept her eyes on him. Dayton wasn't smiling. Something was wrong.

"What is it?" she asked.

Kneeling in front of her, Dayton took both of her hands in his and after placing a quick kiss on her fabric covered belly, saluting his sons, he raised his eyes to hers.

"I know that, for a long time, you have been trying to find your biological father. We looked through tons of folders and files and didn't find much. Then, the family of your mother's attorney sent over three big boxes of folders. We agreed that because of the sensitive nature of some of the documents, we would let someone of legal authority look at them. That ended up being Deputy Sheriff McKenna and Shelton helped too."

"I know all of this," she said, impatiently. "You're taking a long time to get out whatever it is you're trying to say. Now is not the time to be longwinded," Kima joked.

Dayton exhaled, closed his eyes and then opened them again.

"Okay. A while ago, Shelton and McKenna got a lead. He put his private investigator on it and, well, he found your father. He found the man that your mother had been in love with and had you."

Dayton waited. He searched Kima's face for a reaction, but got none.

"Wh...wh..what? You found him? When? How? What?" Kima questioned.

"Yes, baby. He was located. Shelton and McKenna along with Perry went to see him. Do you want to know more? I don't want to upset you on our wedding day. I want to tread lightly here."

"Yes, yes! I want to know. You found him?" she asked again with an extra level of excitement.

This time, Dayton let out a big sigh. Kima was smiling so bright, he was ready to pour it all out in sixty seconds. He decided to still take it slow.

"His name is Niles Hampton. He lives in Miami, Florida. He's been here for about twenty years. He's married and his wife's name is Naomi. They have twin sons who are nineteen years old, Rashad and Quinton Hampton. They also have a little granddaughter, Rashad's daughter and her name is Kylie. She's two. Your father is a partner in a law firm. His wife is a professor at the University of Miami, where both sons currently attend. When Shelton and Perry met with him, they said he cried. He knew about you, but was told that the two of you, you and your mother, died years ago. You'll never guess who delivered that information to him," he asked.

Kima couldn't imagine a person alive who would do that. Then she did know.

"Oscar," she muttered under her breath.

"Yes. We were able to get from Niles that he and your mother met on a beach in Brazil. He worked at a food stand. He didn't know a lot about her, but they did conceive you. Things were going well until word came that Hydea's father had died. She never knew him, as you already know. She was whisked away and he never saw her again. He didn't learn until a few years later that she had been pregnant. Even more years later, he tried looking for the two of you. He had limited funds, so that didn't turn out well. One day, Oscar showed up out of the blue with some papers that said you were dead. That was that. Niles went with what he was told. Oscar did that so that he could work his way into Hydea's life and money. He heard that someone was trying to find her. When he found out who it was, he cooked up a scheme to keep Niles away for good."

"By telling him we were dead! Oh, my god – Oscar is a sanctimonious bastard!" she shouted.

"Yes, baby, he is. The good thing is, he's out of our lives for good now."

Kima began to cry and Dayton reached for a napkin. He would have to get Brielle back in to touch up her makeup.

"How terrible. I lived with that man for years and called him dad," she sniffled.

"I know, baby. I know. McKenna was able to get Shelton in to see Oscar, who remains in prison in Australia on numerous charges. He confessed to not only killing your mother, but of also hiring the men who killed the lawyer. In the boxes the lawyer's family sent us was a packet with proof of his killing your mother. That's what Oscar was trying to get out of the lawyer who wouldn't tell him anything. He's in jail singing like a canary, burying a lot of others involved in criminal activity. It won't get him out of jail, but he declared if he was going down, he wouldn't do it alone."

"This is a lot, Dayton. It's too much," she cried.

"Do you want me to stop? I don't want this to be a downer today of all days," he explained.

"No, no. I want to know all about my father. Did he ask about me? Does he want to meet me? I know you kept this from me to not hurt me if it didn't turn out well. I love you for all that you and your family have done. I just want to know what was said," she pleaded.

Dayton held her hands tighter.

"Okay, I don't want you getting all wired up. We've had enough complications with the twins and the doctor said one more week and they're coming out. The biggest part is yet to be told."

"You're so dramatic. Tell me!" she screamed and shook his shoulders.

"He's here, Kima. Niles, his wife, the boys and their grandbaby are here. Along with them are Niles' two brothers and their families, his three sisters and their families and his father, your grandfather. They are all here on the ranch. They arrived this morning. I wanted to surprise you with them for our wedding. I needed to be sure they could make it before I told you. I didn't want you to continue thinking that you didn't have family other than my family. The moment we were able to confirm through blood tests that he was your father, he was ready to hop on a plane immediately. That was about three weeks ago. Today, if you want, he is here to walk his daughter down the aisle to put her hand in mine. Most of all, he's here because he has a daughter and no matter how old you are or will get, you have him and the rest of the family. Let me just say that, when you see your brothers, don't be frightened. You could be triplets."

On that, Dayton felt his own tears shed for the biggest, happiest smile on Kima's face that he's ever seen. When she grabbed him and kissed his face before pulling him in for as tight a hug as she could get with her protruding stomach in the way, they cried together. After several minutes, they pulled away.

"Where is he? I want to see him."

"I'm right here, Kima."

Kima looked up as a very tall, distinguished man filled the doorway of the room. At first look, she thought she was looking at actor Richard Lawson, who was married to entertainer Beyonce's mother, Tina Knowles. Their features were awfully similar.

Dayton stood and helped her stand. Her eyes never left her father's. She had waited, what seemed a lifetime to find him. Dayton and his family had done this for her.

"Baby, this is Niles Hampton, your father," Dayton said.

"Correction," Niles offered. "Her dad."

Nothing would have prevented Kima from doing what she had longed to do all of her life. She went into the outstretched arms of her father. From this moment on, with Dayton, their sons, his family and now her newfound family, she was whole.

Dayton walked quietly out of the room, closed the

door and let them have their moment. When he reached the bottom of the stairs, he was greeted by his mother and father. They too were already dressed for the wedding, but knew that he had to let Kima and her dad have this moment.

"You did good, son. I'm so proud of you," David said.

"I'm trying not to cry. Brielle will already have to re-do Kima's makeup," Marta joked as David wiped a few unshed tears from her eyes with his handkerchief.

"She's alright?" David asked.

"She's perfect, Pop. You know, my life has come full circle to a point that I can finally start my life again, this time on the right track. I thought that was going to be racing until I was too old to drive. I thought I would find my true purpose and life-filling moments away from Bozeman. The moment I met Kima and she showed me what my heart needed, I knew I would find a new purpose. I still love racing as I do today, but it has a different meaning. It's not about the speed and the rush I get coming in first place. Now, it's about being first in Kima's eyes and those of our children. She and those boys have given me a new purpose. The idea of family first that you have always taught us brought me back here. I hated that it was something bad that sent me running back here, but it had to happen for me to get to this place. I can still do what I love while still staying close to the family. Being home around everyone doesn't get any better than this. I've been working hands-on with the new track, far enough away that the noise of racing won't travel this far, but still close enough to home that I can be with my family in minutes. Shelton's company is going to start construction of our new, bigger home in a month and every morning when I wake, I'm thankful that the right track for me is the one that leads to all of you. Thanks for always being what I need when I need it. Thanks for never giving up on me."

"Day, whatever and wherever life was going to take you, we were always going to be here. The best part of all that has happened is that you have found your life here in Bozeman, on this ranch and you've brought Kima and her family into our fold. This, son, is what Sullivans do," David said.

"Have a seat and let Kima take as long as she likes. We're about to have another Sullivan wedding on this property, so this is a glorious day!" Marta exclaimed.

Dayton smiled as his mother headed toward the front door followed by his father. He then took a seat in the family room. He didn't care if Kima and her dad took all day, she is worth the wait. He was happy that Shelton and McKenna didn't give up on finding Kima's father. He didn't want her to go the rest of her life thinking that the man Oscar was, the father figure she'd known her whole life is how fathers are with their children.

Everything he'd learned about Niles was good stuff. Dayton smiled now knowing where Kima's dream of becoming a lawyer came from. It's in her genes. Knowing that her family will only be a plane ride away gives him hope that anything is possible. Finding purpose in life and getting it on track was a priority. He was glad that he discovered that early enough in his life that he could turn things around and fine true happiness.

Epilogue
Three months later

"Give me my nephew," Shelton said, reaching for Austin who was screaming at the top of his lungs as Dayton changed Dustin's pamper. He had stopped by Dayton's house to talk about whether the design for the new house should include more than five bedrooms and six bathrooms.

Dayton was having the best day looking after both boys. As much as he was looking forward to the new house, his love for his sons was all he could focus on these days.

What he and Kima had originally decided on was not that many bedrooms. They had been thinking more along the lines of four bedrooms and five bathrooms. That had been the original plan before the twins were born. He knew that Kima proclaimed that the twins would not be their only children. She wanted many more. Dayton wasn't surprised and didn't mind. As his wife, who was currently sleeping, she controlled the number of babies. He would be happy about them all. leaving Dayton to look after the three-month-old twins.

Reaching into the crib that was setup in the living room, Shelton picked up Austin who immediately stopped crying.

"I see you have a way with babies the same way you do with women. Speaking of women, how is McKenna doing?" Dayton asked.

"Your daddy has jokes," Shelton responded, taking to Austin.

"Seriously, are you going to tell me what's been going on with the two of you? I haven't said anything because these boys keep me busy when I try to give Kima extra time to rest. Two babies at once is no joke. They take up all of our time, as they should."

"What? Are they interrupting your alone time with your wife? Is she back to alone time yet? I know it's been three months."

"It's still tricky, but you know you Perry and Nick taught me all of your ways, you great sensei's!" Dayton kidded. "There are many ways around any and everything traditional, including that.

"At least give her the rest of the year or so before you pop out more babies. You run the risk of more twins. Now, we know where the twin thing comes from; Kima's side of the family. How is her family? I know they were here for the wedding and then for the birth of the twins. I was out of town when that happened. Things still good?"

Dayton nodded and giggled at Dustin whose legs were kicking and moving like he was fighting someone.

"Yeah, they are really good. Her brothers are actually coming next weekend for a visit. Her father either calls her every day or she calls him. Her stepmother, well her mother, as Kima keeps reminding me to call her, was on the phone with mom when I was at the house yesterday. She has some great ideas for helping mom expand the school here with her being a college professor and all. It's all good and Kima is happier than she's ever been. Now, back to you and McKenna; Deputy Sheriff McKenna. Does she like you to call her that in bed? I know you're tapping that. I've seen her car, even her patrol car, at your condo a lot of times. I knew something was up when I saw her at the wedding. She cleans up nice!" Dayton said.

Shelton did speak, but gave him a thumbs up.

Dayton had never seen his brother this wrapped up in one woman. For years, women called him a black heart. It wasn't because he was mean on intolerable to them. There wasn't a woman alive who had anything bad to say about him other than he wouldn't commit to any of them. He was called, "the black heart" because he said there would never be a woman who could turn his heart read signifying love. He wasn't the love kind of guy.

"Bro, you have no idea. We started out working on that stuff around Kima for you. When Marcus got tied up and he assigned the checks into Oscar to her, we sort of fell into a routine. Then we flirted. Then we danced one night out at a club on a night when she was off and we both ended up there. All I can say is, later that night, she came back to my place and brought her handcuffs.

Man, it was on! Whew!" Shelton yelped. The sound made Austin chuckle and wiggle.

"I can't get that out of all of the people in this family and on this ranch, Austin likes you better than anyone; even me," Dayton proclaimed.

"That's because he knows his uncle will always have his back. I bet you can't wait to teach them how to ride."

"Oh, I can wait, but I will. You can't live on the ranch and not love riding something whether it's horses or cars. They will learn to love ranch life the way we all have. So, you and McKenna an item? I haven't heard any crass stories lately about your escapades with other women."

"We've got something happening. It's caught me by surprise, but yeah, there is something there. Before you joke me on it, I know what I've always declared. I do like her. I'm thinking about coming clean with the family over Sunday dinner by inviting her. Most suspect, but no one other than you, really knows."

"What? That's big for you," Dayton said handing Dustin to Shelton while he grabbed their bottles. Any minute now, as hunger sets in, there will be two babies taking the roof off the house with their hunger pains. He knew he had to hurry to keep them from waking Kima up. She does most of the work with the boys when he's working.

"I know. She's becoming really special to me. In fact, I'm going to head out in a few minutes."

"I thought you may be a business meeting or something. You know you don't have to wear a suit all the time. Shirt, tie, cuffs, sunglasses matching. Dark gray suit, gray expensive shoes. You looking like a walking advertisement for male models," Dayton said, looking at his attire.

"Hey, you do me and I will do me. The suits are my signature look; you know that. I stopped by just to chat about the house and to see my nephews. I can't wait to buy them suits to match their uncle. They are going to be the coolest babies alive!" Shelton decreed.

"I already told Kima to prepare for that. I had a feeling you'd take a specific liking to them," Dayton chuckled.

"Anyway, once you have these two new Sullivans setup for their next meal, I'm going to head out. I just needed to know about the house. I'm meeting Marcus in a few minutes. I think he's thinking about leaving the Sheriff's office and getting into something else. Did you know he has a degree in finance? I had no idea. We're going to talk about a role for him in my company. I think the selling point was that he could make four times what he makes now. He wanted to hear more."

Dayton noticed a difference in Marcus. Now he knew why.

"Marcus is a great guy. He and Perry have been friends for a lot of years. I think over the past few years, they've been more of best friends. I have noticed that Marcus comes around the ranch a lot more these days than ever," Dayton said.

"He bought a horse. He doesn't have the proper setup to keep a horse at his house, so he comes here every day, just to check on and ride his horse. So, the house?" Shelton asked.

Dayton forgot as he placed the boys in their crib and placed a bottle in each of their mouths. They immediately start feeding as if they were starving. He would never tire of the sight before him.

"The house. Let's add two more bedrooms and one more bath. I also want a larger room on the second floor to be a playroom for the kids, not a bedroom though. No outlets or any other dangers. It needs to be kid-friendly," Dayton explained.

Shelton stood to leave.

"Alright, bro. I got it. I'll email you a new layout tonight. Construction will begin in about another month."

"That works. Hey, I hope to see McKenna at Sunday dinner. She makes you happy. That's a good look for you," Dayton encouraged.

Shelton waved at him as he opened the front door.

"We shall see," he said stepping out. "I'm going to go see Perry and Gizelle's baby girl, then I'll be off the ranch for a few days. You know how to reach me if you need me."

Shelton shut the door and raced down the steps to his truck. Putting the truck in drive, he turned on his radio as a special news alert came over the air.

'*Again, we repeat, there was an attempted bank robbery in downtown Bozeman today. One Deputy Sheriff is in grave condition and is being airlifted to a major hospital outside of Bozeman. Another Deputy Sheriff was also shot and has been taken to Bozeman Health Deaconess Hospital. We will keep you abreast of the situation as we learn more.*'

A dark cloud covered Shelton's mood. The minute his phone rang and he saw Marcus' number, he prepared to hear the worst.

"How bad is she?" Shelton asked before giving Marcus a chance to speak.

"You heard? She's the one that was taken to our local hospital. She's bad, but not as bad as Khalil. He was hit three times."

"I'm on my way," Shelton alerted him as he sped toward the entrance to the ranch. He hoped the gates were already open because he wasn't planning on stopping long enough to wait. He would hate to ruin his latest purchase, his new dark green Jaguar F-type Heritage 60 edition, by ramming the front gate, but he would.

"Shelton, before you get to the hospital, I need to warn you about something that I don't think you know," Marcus asserted.

Shelton couldn't take any more bad news, especially if it was about McKenna. He and Dayton had just been talking about her. He held back on how he really felt about her because he had been keeping their time together a secret from everyone until he figured out what it was himself. Hearing that she was injured sent his head on a whirlwind. All he knew was that he needed to see her for himself to see how bad she was hurt.

"What is it?" Shelton huffed out.

"I don't know how to hit you with this, so I'm just going to blurt it out. Shelton, McKenna's mother and father are on their way."

When Marcus stopped, Shelton lost his patience. He knew there was more but for some reason, Marcus hesitated sharing it.

"Marcus, stop stalling. What's going on? I know she has a mother and father. I would assume if she was hurt in the line of duty that her parents would be the first people you would call. What is it that you're not saying?" he asked.

"Also, on the way here is...McKenna's husband. She's married, Shelton. He's on his way to Bozeman as we speak," Marcus explained.

Just before he reached the gates of the ranch, which were already being opened for him, Shelton slammed on the breaks. He could not have heard Marcus clearly.

"What the hell are you talking about her husband? She's married? What the hell, Marcus?" Shelton shouted.

With his car stopped, Shelton swiped his hand across his face to focus on what had just been revealed to him.

"McKenna is married to a career serviceman. He's on his way to Bozeman. You didn't know?"

"Hell, no! I wouldn't have fallen..."

Shelton caught himself. In the height of the moment, he was about to say the words that had been dazzling his tongue for a few weeks.

"What? Say it. You wouldn't have fallen in love with her if you knew she was married. Trust me, McKenna feels the same way."

"She can't. She can't love two men equally. She played me, Marcus. She has a whole-ass husband and never said a word. You know about us, so you know what's been going on. I never would have if I had known she was married. I can't tell you how many chances she had to tell me before..."

Shelton didn't have to explain what *'before'* meant. He knew that Marcus already knew.

"Are you still coming to the hospital?" Marcus asked.

"Three's a crowd. I gotta go."

Shelton was pissed. He needed some space; he needed a lot of space.

Instead of heading to the hospital where he would probably embarrass himself and run into McKenna's husband, he turned his car in a different direction and headed for his condo.

"I'm freakin' *done* with women," he screamed and banged his fist on the steering wheel. "They don't want a loyal brother; I was fine being a playboy. It's time I found that guy again," he shouted through clinched teeth.

As much as he was hurting by not going to the hospital, he can't believe McKenna has been lying to him for months. She had many chances to tell him she was married.

As he drove, a bit faster than he should, Shelton's phone pinged with a text message. He pulled over to read it seeing that it's coming from McKenna's phone. To his dismay, it wasn't her; it was her best friend and fellow Deputy Sheriff, Tessa Curley using McKenna's phone.

'Shelton, it's Tessa. McKenna wanted me to reach out to you before you heard about what happened to her. She's pretty sure you know by now. There is more that you have to know. Can you please call me so that I can explain for her? She also said you will hear some things about her that are not true. They had to sedate her, so that's all she said. Call me and I will explain. You have to call me before you come to the hospital. I'm sorry, but you won't like what you hear. Call me.'

Shelton threw his phone on the seat next to him and repeated what he said to Marcus; three's a crowd. He was going home. What he wouldn't be doing is talking to any third person who could explain to him what McKenna could or would not. If she had secrets, he thought that they were close enough that she should have felt comfortable enough telling him.

He drove and thought back to the days and nights of testing their sexual boundaries. There were also days and nights of steamy, hot and passionate encounters. All of them got better and better with time; time that he now knew was a lie. Whatever McKenna or her friend had to say, he didn't want to hear it. She had no idea that before her, he never thought he'd let a woman get as close to him as he allowed her to get. He had to get back to that guy women called, 'the black heart'. He never should have changed from that. He thought McKenna was worth him making that change. He guessed karma was paying him a visit and he didn't like it. He didn't like it one bit.

Get Shelton and McKenna's story, Three's a Crowd, the fourth book in the Sullivans of Montana series. It's available now for preorder at www.cherylbarton.net

Three's a Crowd
The Sullivans of Montana, Book 4

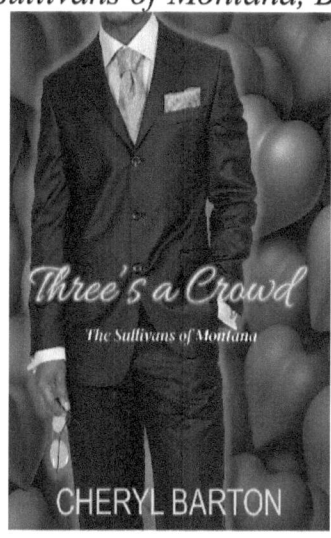

Businessman Shelton Sullivan was clear that as a kid, he loved life growing up on the Sullivan Ranch wrangling cattle and riding horses. As a man, he prefers big city life, wrangling expensive suits and most of all, riding sexy women. He was blindsided when a woman penetrated the wall of steel that surrounded, what some said was his black heart, when it came to being in love; he preferred lust.

Deputy Sheriff McKenna Gibson needed a fresh start in a new city. Escaping a life that was crafted for her had become old and dull. Sizzling, spicy encounters with Bozeman's most eligible bachelor was exactly what she needed to help her forget the secrets she was hoping to leave behind in her old life as a military wife.

Without warning, Shelton found himself swept up

into McKenna's amorous sensualities that very much matched his own dalliances. Their steamy, seductive encounters led to even more explicit and erotic romps until Shelton's world crashed down like a Montana boulder. McKenna is injured in the line of duty and his world is rocked off of its axis when her military husband blew up the love he thought was blossoming from the one time he decided to let down his guard.

Is Shelton willing to forgive and forget and turn away from the red-hot stirring in his chest at the thought of her?

"Home for Thanksgiving"
Book 1 of The Sullivans of Montana

Firefighter Nicholas Sullivan is going home for the holiday after he was sidelined due to an injury on the job. Guilt over a life lost has kept him away from his family's ranch in Montana and now he's forced to face his past demons and deal with a self-imposed life of regret.

Veterinarian Parker Wingate's first encounter with the handsome firefighter was less than pleasurable. She sympathized with his hurt, understood his pain and before long, felt his love.

Knowing the holiday season is ending soon, can Nick go from living in love for the moment to allowing himself to finally live in love forever?

The Way You Love Me
Book 2 of The Sullivans of Montana

Montana ranch owner, Perry Sullivan, befriended a woman who finds herself in dire need of his help. He doesn't hesitate to provide shelter and protection the way any man should for a woman who is in distress.

What he had not planned on was in the midst of the turmoil that was her life, he would lose his heart and fall in love while at the same time putting the lives of his own family at risk.

Gizelle Duncan had a tumultuous past she didn't want anyone to know about, but when that past, in the form of her abusive ex-husband, shows up in her life again, she has no choice but to accept help from one of those sexy Sullivan boys from the Sullivan Ranch. She thought she had lost all faith in real love until Perry showed her that she could trust him not only with her life, but with her heart.

The Way You Love Me will take you on a journey from the ashes of Gizelle's burned-out house and life and into the flames of passion that will not be contained even at the peril of a jealous ex-husband out for revenge.

An Unexpected Destiny
Sister Act Series, Book 1

Now available!

Destiny Lockhart's high school crush, Lincoln Cole, is again front and center in her life. She last saw him fifteen years ago when she threw him out of her bedroom after their one night together following the senior prom. That night had been her most embarrassing moment, leaving her feeling ashamed and undesirable.

There was no way entertainment mogul Lincoln Cole could ever forget the shy, yet beautiful butterfly that was Destiny from his years as a high school football star. The now feisty, sexy and self-confident executive who dripped in vibrant, dazzling appeal reminded him that they were never meant to only have a one-night-stand. They were always destined for forever.

For years, they lived on two different coasts unaware that soon, their past would become an unexpected present filled with unfinished desires that once looked like rejection.

***If you enjoyed, An Unexpected Destiny,
book one of the "Sister Act" series, you are
going to love book 2, For You I Will***

Kasey Young discovered that a man would do anything to keep her in his grips, even if it's her ex-husband. She lived her life his way for years until she'd had enough and filed for divorce. He wants to insert himself back into her life with an ultimatum; take him back or lose custody of their kids. Kasey found herself between a rock and a hard place needing the help of a man she barely knew, but who stirred up deep carnal desires that had been lying dormant.

Attorney Darren Braxton stepped up to the plate to help Kasey with her child custody case as a favor for a friend. What he hadn't planned on was the hedonistic lust for a woman who could cause him to lose all he's gained because he can't say no to her. He did the one thing he could think of to save them both; he married her.

asey has to convince the court that their love is real or she could lose everything. Could she before it's too late?

The Christmas Layover

Millionaire Edrick Stone's plan to spend the Christmas holiday alone at his villa in Spain was derailed by a sudden snowstorm that hit Denver, Colorado just as he was leaving. He couldn't be mad at the storm when he discovered a friendly passenger across the aisle was also stranded, much to his delight.

Danica hated Christmas; even her friends secretly called her Scrooge. She carried a secret pain that resurfaced each year with the holiday until a mysterious stranger on a plane offered her the chance to have a very merry Christmas. She decided to throw caution to the wind and live in the moment.

Edrick and Danica had their own reasons for avoiding Christmas, but this year, they would find that the holiday wasn't meant to be spent alone, but in arms filled with love and possibilities.

It Should Have Been You

Karma:

Dr. Clayton Myers was never a believer in karma, but he did believe in fate. Both would soon collide and expose a secret that would impact the perfect life and relationship with the only woman he ever loved, but not the only woman he took to his bed. That revelation would put his life on a path he accepted while never forgetting what could have been.

Disappointment:

Dr. Donna Spencer had experienced one of the darkest days of her life at the hands of the man who made a promise of forever. She took the hit to her heart and realized nothing good lasts forever.

Fate:

After years of no contact, Clayton and Donna's paths would cross again, forcing them to face the past where their love resided, while wondering what should have been and if they could find their way back to love again.

The Power of Seduction

Bakery owner Raquel Hastings assumed her relationship was perfect in every way, both in and out of the bedroom where she had enjoyed the most tempting, titillating, and out-of-this-world sensual romps between the sheets with sexy engineer, Preston Sharpe, a man who knows his way around a woman's body. That was until he took a job in another country which left her only with memories and intoxicating desires to be loved like that again. Her world had been turned upside down until the day he returned with a plan to turn her world right side up.

Preston's alluring visions of Raquel haunted him at night, alone in his bed in a foreign country without the woman he loved. With the chance to return home and to her loving arms, he dreamed of once again sharing nights of satiating passion that only two hearts meant for each other could share. He knew he had to ready his game of seduction if he were ever going to again have Raquel back in his life and in his bed. This time, his plan was to make it last forever with the hope that Raquel could forgive him and give their love another chance.

Read it for free on Kindle Unlimited!
https://www.amazon.com/dp/B09LSLFG6D

Make sure you check out book 1, of "The Brothers of Chi-Town", *I Can't Let Go* – now available for download and in paperback.

I Can't Let Go

Carter Garrison vowed to love, honor and cherish his wife, Sienna, forsaking all others, something he forgot to do during a weekend of fun, bad company and poor judgement.

Sienna Garrison never dreamed her college sweetheart, Carter, whom she pledged her life to, would break her heart and when he did, she moved out and moved on - or tried to.

What better occasion is there than a friend's wedding to stir up old feelings and memories of love, intense passion and nights of sensual titillation. Gazes from across a room after almost two years apart revealed depths of love that had never died.

Seeing Sienna again reminded Carter of what he'd lost and he vowed to never let go by doing whatever he could to get his wife back even if it included begging and pleading. Is Sienna ready to forgive and take a chance on life again with the only man she'd ever really loved?

When Carter brings on the charm and turns up the heat, no woman is immune, especially Sienna.

Don't forget to snag your copy of book 2, *Swagger and Baggage*, in "The Brothers of Chi-Town" series – now available

Swagger and Baggage

It's not a coincidence that casino owner, Torrence Allen, ran into his college sweetheart, Reese Michaels again; it's fate. As his memories unfold, he had tried everything to keep her in his life and his bed back then and failed at both. She wasn't ready for him then, but he hopes she is ready for him now.

Reese Michaels never thought she'd see Torrence again. Their split in college was dramatic and hurtful and still, no man had been able to win her heart. She considered herself the permanent third wheel to friends who had found love and marriage.

Torrence's swagger has always won women over, but it's his baggage that's causing his life to spiral out of control. He messed up and found himself without the woman he has always loved.